She stopped 

ne of the rooms. D ating so hard that ntion and walked straight into the back of her.

Her body weight shot forward, her hands still clutching the clipboard, with no time to try and break her fall as her feet started to disconnect from the floor. The green rubber floor loomed beneath her eyes.

A warm arm grabbed her around the waist with such intensity that her breath was taken clean away from her. She was yanked back hard—straight into the chest of Donovan Reid.

'Grace, I'm sorry. I wasn't paying attention.'

She couldn't speak for a few seconds. All the air had shot out of her lungs. When she finally managed to suck in a breath and relax back against him all she could do was laugh.

It was a nervous laugh. An *I'm-feeling-something-I-shouldn't* kind of laugh.

Like the heat of someone else's warm skin seeping straight through her thin scrubs. The feel of the rise and fall of his chest muscles against her shoulder blades. She should have kept her dress and her heels on. The thicker material and a little more height wouldn't have left her quite so exposed. She could feel the outline of other parts of his body too.

His hand was still locked around her waist, holding her close to him. It didn't matter that he'd already seen every part of her. It didn't matter that she'd been naked in a shower with him. This was up close and personal. This felt even more intimate than that.

Dear Reader

This is the third story I've set in my fictional Disease Prevention Agency. You might have guessed by now that I love everything about infectious diseases and immunisation campaigns—which is probably why I've ended up working in Public Health for the last nine years.

This story is about Donovan Reid, the resident hunk at the DPA, who was briefly mentioned in THE MAVERICK DOCTOR AND MISS PRIM and noted for his ambition and drive.

Grace Barclay has only been at the DPA for seven months. She's finished her residency and is trying to gain a coveted place on one of the fieldwork teams. Then one day she opens an envelope at work and everything changes…

For this story I've used the Marburg Virus. You might not have heard of it, but it's the disease they based the film *Outbreak* on. I watched that film again recently, and was very amused to see the resident hunk of *Grey's Anatomy*, Patrick Dempsey, looking very young and being bitten by a monkey. I had totally forgotten he was in it!

The most fun I had with this book was trying to write a sexy, emotional kind of scene with two people dressed in the equivalent of space suits!

I love to hear from readers. You can contact me via my website, www.scarlet-wilson.com, follow me on Twitter @scarlet_wilson, or find me on Facebook at the Scarlet Wilson Author Page.

Hope you enjoy Grace and Donovan's story!

Scarlet Wilson

TEMPTED BY HER BOSS

BY
SCARLET WILSON

First published in Great Britain 2014
by Mills & Boon, an imprint of Harlequin (UK) Limited,
Large Print edition 2015
Eton House, 18-24 Paradise Road,
Richmond, Surrey, TW9 1SR

ISBN: 978-0-263-25456-3

Harlequin (UK) Limited's policy is to use papers that are natural, renewable and recyclable products and made from wood grown in sustainable forests. The logging and manufacturing processes conform to the legal environmental regulations of the country of origin.

Printed and bound in Great Britain
by CPI Antony Rowe, Chippenham, Wiltshire

Scarlet Wilson wrote her first story aged eight and has never stopped. Her family have fond memories of *Shirley and the Magic Purse*, with its army of mice, all with names beginning with the letter 'M'. An avid reader, Scarlet started with every Enid Blyton book, moved on to the *Chalet School* series and many years later found Mills & Boon®.

She trained and worked as a nurse and health visitor, and currently works in public health. For her, finding Medical Romances™ was a match made in heaven. She is delighted to find herself among the authors she has read for many years.

Scarlet lives on the West Coast of Scotland with her fiancé and their two sons.

Recent Mills & Boon® Medical Romance™ titles by Scarlet Wilson:

A MOTHER'S SECRET
200 HARLEY STREET: GIRL FROM THE RED CARPET†
HER FIREFIGHTER UNDER THE MISTLETOE
ABOUT THAT NIGHT…**
THE MAVERICK DOCTOR AND MISS PRIM**
AN INESCAPABLE TEMPTATION
HER CHRISTMAS EVE DIAMOND
A BOND BETWEEN STRANGERS*
WEST WING TO MATERNITY WING!
THE BOY WHO MADE THEM LOVE AGAIN
IT STARTED WITH A PREGNANCY

†*200 Harley Street*
**The Most Precious Bundle of All*
***Rebels with a Cause*

Recent Mills & Boon® Cherish™ titles by Scarlet Wilson:

THE HEIR OF THE CASTLE
ENGLISH GIRL IN NEW YORK

Dedication

This book is dedicated to my dad,
John Niven Wilson, who tells me that
everything I write is wonderful and encourages me
to do the best I can. I challenge anyone to
find a man with as much integrity as my dad.

This book is also dedicated to my mum,
Joanne Barrie Wilson, the woman with the best
singing voice I know, who has spent her life
putting her family first. There aren't enough words
for how much my sisters and I love you!

Praise for Scarlet Wilson:

'HER CHRISTMAS EVE DIAMOND
is a fun and interesting read. If you like a sweet
romance with just a touch of the holiday season
you'll like this one.'
—*HarlequinJunkie*

'WEST WING TO MATERNITY WING!
is a tender, poignant and highly affecting romance
that is sure to bring a tear to your eye.
With her gift for creating wonderful characters, her
ability to handle delicately and compassionately
sensitive issues and her talent for writing
believable, emotional and spellbinding romance,
the talented Scarlet Wilson continues to
prove to be a force to be reckoned with in the
world of contemporary romantic fiction!'
—*CataRomance*

CHAPTER ONE

'DONOVAN REID IS sex on legs,' sighed Grace as she gathered up the remains of her lunch. Her two colleagues mumbled in agreement, too busy watching the object of their admiration through the glass window to the workout room.

It really wasn't fair. How was anyone supposed to concentrate on their lunch when they had a view like that?

His light brown curly hair was wet with perspiration, his running vest and shorts allowing every sculpted muscle to be on display as his legs pounded on the running machine. The look on his was face intense, as if every single thing on this planet depended on him reaching his goal. The machine started to slow and he blinked in recognition, decreasing his pace and picking up the towel on the handrail to dry around his face and neck.

This was their Friday lunchtime ritual. Come down to the staffroom and goggle at Donovan Reid. Their local Matthew McConaughey look-alike.

Lara dumped her half-eaten sandwich in the trash, her eyes flickering between Grace and Dr Gorgeous. 'How long is it since you've had a date, Grace?'

'Don't start.'

Lara folded her arms across her chest. 'No, really. What happened to the computer guy?'

Grace shook her head; she could feel the hackles going up at the back of her neck. 'Leave it, Lara.' She wasn't about to tell her friends that dating just freaked her out. Everything was fine in a busy, crowded restaurant. But take her out of that situation and into a one on one and a whole pile of irrational fears raised their heads.

'Are you going to tell me what happened?'

'Nothing happened. We went on a few dates but that was it. Nothing.' It was simpler not to date. She just didn't want to say that out loud. They would be rushing her down the corridor to the nearest counsellor and that she could do without.

She just needed a little time. She would be fine. She would.

Lara nodded her head at the glistening muscles of Donovan Reid, who was towelling himself off before heading to the showers. 'So, have you considered any other options?'

Grace rolled her eyes. 'Oh, get real, Lara. The guy doesn't even know I exist. Have you seen the kind of women he normally dates?'

Anna piped in, 'Oh, yeah, blondes, big Amazonian types.'

They turned to look at her.

She shrugged. 'What? I saw him out at dinner the other week.'

'And you never mentioned it?' Lara seemed annoyed.

'Why would I? He never even recognised me. Believe me, he was otherwise occupied.'

Grace looked down at her own curvy body, visions of Donovan Reid wrapped around some lithe blonde model plaguing her mind, then back through the glass towards him. 'Well, I guess that rules me out, then.' She tossed her water bottle in the recycling bin, but her eyes were drawn straight back to Donovan like a magnet. She just couldn't stop staring. Maybe it was the safety aspect. Donovan Reid was in the 'unattainable' category for her. Plus there was the fact she already knew how he'd reacted in a similar situation to hers. He'd come out of it unscathed. It kind of helped with his hero persona. 'The DPA should have one of those calendars. You know, the charity kind with a naked man for every month? Think of the money we could raise for charity.'

Lara laughed. 'And apart from Donovan, who are we going to get to model for it? We're kind of short of handsome men around here.'

Anna smiled. 'That's okay. I could easily look at a different picture of Donovan every month.' She tilted her head to the side as the three of them turned to appreciate their prey once more.

He'd finished in the gym and was grabbing his gear and heading to the showers.

Grace sighed. It was official. His butt was her favourite part of him.

It had been seven months since they'd finished their residencies and started at the Disease Prevention Agency. The DPA had over one thousand five hundred employees in Atlanta alone, with another ten thousand across the US and fifty other countries worldwide. Grace and her colleagues were currently part of the two-year training programme within the Emerging Disease branch of the DPA. Two years to learn everything they needed to know about preventing disease, disability and death from infectious diseases.

Placements included lab work, epidemiology, contact tracing, public health statistics and fieldwork. Some of the placements were exciting, some mundane, but the glimpse of Donovan Reid's butt was often the highlight of Grace's long twelve-hour-shift day.

'Where are you covering this afternoon?' she asked Anna.

'I'm down in the labs. What about you?'

She shook her head. 'I'm on the phones. Crazy bat lady, here I come.'

Lara hadn't moved. She was still watching Donovan's retreating back. 'You know there's a place going on his team, don't you?'

'What?' Both heads turned in unison.

Lara nodded. 'Yeah, Mhairi Spencer's pregnant. She won't be covering fieldwork any more.'

It made sense. A few years before, one of the DPA staff had died from an ectopic pregnancy in a far-off land. That was the trouble with working for the Disease Prevention Agency. A field assignment could mean staff would be miles from the nearest hospital. The weird and wonderful diseases they covered didn't often appear in built-up areas. Regulations had been reviewed and it had been decided that as soon as any member of staff discovered they were pregnant, fieldwork was a no-no.

The tiny hairs on Grace's arms stood on end. This was it. The chance she'd been waiting for. Seven months she'd been at the DPA, desperately waiting for the opportunity to get on one of the field teams. And to be on a team with the resident hunk? Wow.

The trouble was, the same thought was mirrored on her friends' faces. She could almost hear the sound of whirring as their brains started frantically calculating the best way to make the team.

She held out her fist. They'd all started here

together. They were friends. And this was their little show of unity. 'May the best girl win.' Lara and Anna held out their fists so that all three were one on top of the other.

Lara gave a wink. 'Time to fight dirty, girls.'

Grace was trying to appear casual, trying to appear calm. But it wasn't working. Since she'd arrived back at her seat she'd been making frantic notes. Things she could put on her résumé if they asked for one. Conversations she could try and have with Donovan Reid to let him know she would be the best person for his team.

She blew her bangs out of her eyes and leaned back in her chair. Who was she trying to kid? Donovan Reid had never had a conversation with her. He barely knew she existed. Her eyes focused on the sign above the phone. 'NORMAL PEOPLE DON'T PHONE THE DPA.' Didn't she know it?

Ten calls in the last hour. Six from people who had rashes that they thought ranged from bubonic plague to scarlet fever. The other four from healthcare professionals who had patients they couldn't diagnose. The internet was a wonderful thing. These days she could ask callers to take a picture and send it to her, giving them a diagnosis or reassurance in a matter of seconds.

She glanced at her watch. Crazy bat lady was late today. She'd usually phoned in by now. It was always the same conversation. Could the bats nestling in the nearby woods and caves be rabid? What kind of diseases could they carry? What would happen if she came in contact with bat droppings? All the doctors who manned the phones at the DPA knew crazy bat lady, she even greeted some of them by their first names.

Grace turned to the pile of incoming mail. The admin support was off sick. The irony of a sickness and diarrhoea bug sweeping around the DPA headquarters wasn't lost on her. She started opening the brown envelopes and sorting the mail into piles. Lots were lab reports, some queries about different infectious diseases, some journal articles and a few requests from reporters. Nothing too difficult.

The last letter was stuck in the envelope. More difficult to get out than the rest. She gave it a little tug and it finally released, along with a plume of white dust.

The powder flew everywhere like a waft of white smoke, clouding her vision and catching in her throat.

And just like that, everything around her halted.

Donovan heard the collective gasps around him. The office was usually noisy, with a chatter of voices constantly in the background, along with mumbled telephone conversations and the rattle of keyboards.

Every sense went on alert.

He stood up, looking over the top of his pod, his eyes automatically scanning in the direction in which all the heads were pointing.

Was that smoke? No one was allowed to smoke in here. Realisation struck him like a blow to the chest.

That girl. That curvy, gorgeous brunette he'd been meaning to ask a few people about. She was standing stock still with a look of terror on her face. Dust was settling around her, covering her hair, face and clothes with a hazy white powder.

If it had been any other setting, and any other season, she might have looked like she'd just been dusted with the first fall of snow.

But this was the DPA in the middle of autumn. And that was no snow.

Donovan was used to dealing with emergency situations, but they didn't normally occur in his office space. He went into autopilot.

He was the most senior member of staff in the room and the responsibility of implementing safety procedures fell to him. All staff were trained about biohazard risks in the field. But he was already aware by the panicked faces that not everyone would have the quick thinking adaptability to apply them to their own workplace. He had to take the lead.

His long strides took him to the wall where he thumped the red button and the alarm started sounding. 'Everybody, this is not a drill.' His words brought the few people who hadn't already noticed what was happening to their feet. 'Biohazard containment procedures, *now*!'

He kept walking, straight towards his frozen co-worker, racking his brain for her name. Darn it. He should have asked days ago. She was on his list of possibilities for a replacement for Mhairi Spencer. He might not know her name, but he'd noticed her capabilities. Smart. Switched on. And focused. Three essential components.

The last remnant of dust was settling around her. He was walking straight into a potential disaster. But it was far more dangerous to leave her in an office space with circulating air-conditioning. She looked shocked and needed a push in the right direction. He took a breath before he reached her and clamped his mouth shut tight, putting both hands on her shoulders, spinning her round and marching her towards the door.

He didn't speak. He couldn't speak. The risk of inhaling or ingesting the substance was too great. He could only hope she was sensible enough to have stopped breathing.

He glanced sideways at a colleague who pressed the automatic door release, letting the door swing open and Donovan keep his hands in place.

He steered her to the left, nudging another button on the wall with his elbow and heading into the showers he'd just left. The door sealed behind him with a suck of air.

He could hear the motors above him stop. Perfect. The air-conditioning had been switched off. This whole building was designed for a possible disaster—the laboratories downstairs handled a whole range of potentially lethal toxins and pathogens. But this was the first time to his knowledge that there ever been a biohazard via the mail system.

The showers started automatically around them. Steam started to fill the room. 'Strip.'

The word sounded harsh and there was a fleeting second of hesitation in her face before she started to comply, tearing off her shirt and sliding her trousers down over her thighs.

He took the same actions. Pulling off the shirt and tie he'd only replaced ten minutes ago and kicking off his brand-new Italian leather shoes. His designer trousers lay crumpled at his feet. All of these clothes would be incinerated.

It wasn't just her at risk any more, it was him too. And everyone else in the building.

As soon as they were both naked he pulled her

into the showers, grabbing antibacterial scrub and starting to lather it into both their skins.

There was a glazed look in her eyes. She was following instructions but didn't seem to have quite clicked about what had just happened.

There was no room for shyness, no room for subtlety. Everyone in this department knew what to do in the event of exposure to a potential biological threat. Evacuate. Decontaminate staff and area. Isolate any threats. Identify agent. Act accordingly.

He looked at a clock hanging on a nearby wall. 'Fifteen minutes.' The minimum scrub time after exposure.

They had to try and remove every tiny particle from any part of their skin, face, hair and nails. No trace should remain. They couldn't do anything about the particles they might already have inhaled, but further exposure should be eliminated.

Her eyes met his. Caramel brown in this steam-filled room. Her skin was glistening. Her hair was glistening. What was that stuff?

Water was coursing over both their bodies, the

showers set at maximum. He poured some of the antibacterial soap into his hands. 'Come here.' He didn't wait for her to reply, just dumped the soap onto her head and started scrubbing furiously. It was probably some special product she'd deliberately put there and not the mystery powder but he couldn't take that chance.

'What are you doing?' she shrieked. It was the first thing she'd said. It was as if she'd snapped out of her trance. Things were about to get interesting.

The emergency procedures ordered all staff to scrub following exposure, but they certainly didn't imply they should scrub each other. Donovan was improvising. Grace couldn't see the stuff currently glimmering in her hair.

'What do you think I'm doing? I'm trying to get this stuff off you.'

The water and soap ran into her eyes and she spluttered. 'Stop it.' She slapped his hands away. 'I'll do it myself.' She turned her back to him, her first hint of shyness, leaving him with a great view of her curved backside.

'Darn it,' she muttered. 'This stuff will play havoc with my hair.'

He tipped his head back, sloshing water over his face and shampooing his head fiercely. He knew the protocols here. He'd been involved in reviewing them for the last five years. He'd just never expected to have to use them in this set of circumstances.

He started work on his shoulders and arms, rubbing the antibacterial soap over all his body. 'What's your name?' he shouted under the blasting water.

He'd never been naked with a woman whose name he didn't know.

Her head turned and she glowered at him over her shoulder. 'Grace. Grace Barclay.'

He smiled. So that was her name. In a building with one thousand five hundred employees he couldn't possibly know everyone's name. He held his hand out towards her—it was time for official introductions. 'Pleased to meet you, Grace. I'm Donovan Reid.'

She scowled and glared at his hand, making no attempt to take it. 'Oh, don't worry. I know who you are. I've been here for more than seven months.' The water was running over her face and she tilted her head to take it out of the direct stream. 'It would be nice if you could take the trouble to remember your colleagues' names.' She turned her back to him again and started scrubbing her skin.

Feisty. He liked it.

Her long brown hair fell halfway down her back, water streaming down it. He pushed it to one side. 'Let me do your back.' It made sense. She couldn't reach those parts herself and the decontamination protocol was clear. There was no room for shyness at this point in a crisis.

His hand touched her shoulder and he felt her sharp intake of breath under his touch. He started moving his hands, circulating the soap. Her skin was lightly tanned, with white bits in all the right places. And smooth. There was nothing like being naked in the shower with a woman you barely knew. It kind of cut through all the crap.

His hand felt something else and she flinched.

He blinked. Steam was circulating around them. What was that bump in her skin?

It didn't really matter. But the doctor in him—or the man in him—was curious enough to look.

So he did. This time it was his turn to suck in a breath. His fingers moved over the mark—over the scar on her skin. This was no neat surgical scar, this was a rough-edged, deep penetrating wound. A stab wound.

Why would a girl like Grace Barclay have a stab wound? She spun round in the shower. His eyes went automatically to her breasts. He couldn't help it. They were right in front of him. Crying out to be touched. Bigger than he'd noticed, matching the rest of her soft curves.

She could see exactly where he was looking. She folded her arms across her breasts and turned back round.

Caught. Like a kid with his hand in the candy jar. This was getting more interesting by the minute.

Grace was in shock. Naked in a shower with Donovan Reid shock. She couldn't stop her slightly snarky responses. It was as if her automatic defence mechanisms had dropped into place. She couldn't actually believe this was happening.

Because this wasn't real. This *couldn't* be real.

Any fantasies about Donovan Reid having his hands on her body in a shower hadn't been anything like this. Not even close.

No. In those scenarios he'd had her pinned up against a nice glass door with lots of raspberry-smelling bubbles winding their way between their two bodies.

It hadn't resembled anything like this. And for a dream this was pretty awful.

Surely her imagination knew better than to give her a horrible work-related incident?

The hands streaking up and down her back didn't feel sensual, didn't feel gentle. The hands massaging her hair weren't doing it with loving care. They had a purpose. A function.

She cringed as his hands touched her neck and she squeezed her eyes shut. Mr Washboard Abs had a prime view of her big backside and occasionally dimpled thighs right now. Bet none of his Amazonian girlfriends looked like this in the shower. As if they'd just had a battle between a cupcake and a candy bar.

Then they moved. His fingers. And she could almost hear his intake of breath over the pummelling water stream. She couldn't help the natural flinch of her shoulder, pulling her scar away from his fingers. It was inbuilt into her. The permanent reminder of that hideous night.

It didn't matter that this was far removed from that situation. Just the touch of his fingers next to her skin sent her spinning back there. Back to a dark night and an unlit parking lot. The unknown assailant and the struggle for the bag that had been on her shoulder. Why hadn't he just cut the strap? Why did he have to stab her?

Her heart fluttered in her chest. Just what she needed. A run of SVT in the shower with Donovan Reid. Any minute now she'd hit the floor and there would a whole different emergency going on.

She breathed slowly. Controlled breaths. In through her nose and out through her mouth in a long steady stream. The rapid heart rhythm—super ventricular tachycardia—had only occurred a few times since her attack and was always stress induced. Her two fingers reached up to the side of her neck and massaged gently for a few seconds. It didn't take long.

Her heart rate settled, her breathing eased. The tight feeling in her throat released.

Phew. She kept her eyes closed for a few seconds. She had her back to Donovan so he couldn't see her and wouldn't have noticed her manoeuvre.

But he had noticed her scar.

And now she was even more conscious of his touch. Conscious of the fact that the man she dreamed about was inches away from her in a shower. If she leaned back, just a little, she would lean right into his…

Her eyes started open as she felt her body drift backwards. No! She cringed. What must he think of her anyway? First introductions and she'd snapped at him. There was something kind of brutal about a man revealing he'd no idea what your name was. Particularly when you were naked right next to him. Kind of made you realise exactly where you were on his importance scale. Right where you thought—lower than the belly of a snake.

There was no way she was going to be moony eyed around Donovan Reid. She had to remain short, sharp and professional. Just maybe not *quite* so snappy.

It was the shock of the situation. That was all.

Her palms were tingling. Reacting to the feel of his hands on her back, shoulders and neck. If they reached a little lower…

No. Stop it. Anyway, two could play at that game. She was quite sure the protocol hadn't said anything about scrubbing each other's backs. But it did seem practical.

For the first time since she'd got in the shower a smile played around the edges of her lips As she pictured her hands all over Donovan Reid's body. What was it the girls had agreed to earlier? Fight dirty? The thought raced across her mind and quickly back out again.

She'd never do that. She just couldn't even contemplate it. Even with her active imagination. Deep down, that just wasn't her.

She wanted to win her place on his team fair

and square. She'd probably have to be interviewed along with another ten members of staff. But she could do that.

No matter how much he was making her skin tingle, or how much her imagination went into overdrive. Donovan Reid was always professional at work. The last thing he'd be doing right now was having any erotic thoughts about her. Up until a few minutes ago he hadn't even known she existed.

No. Donovan would be contemplating whatever substance the mystery powder was. Just like she should be doing.

Guilt flooded her. Where was her professional responsibility? What about her colleagues out there? It wasn't just her that had been potentially exposed—it had been all of them. Her fingers clawed into her hair, scrubbing for all they were worth. What was the powder? Was it really something dangerous? Could it be an act of terrorism?

The DPA worked worldwide, often leading to some difficult conversations on a global level about their findings. Governments could often take offence when suggestions were made about their contribution to a disease outbreak. Her brain was going into overdrive. The DPA was a US institution. Everyone knew about the work that they did. Maybe someone had decided to make an example of them and hit them with one of the diseases they fought against.

She shuddered. She couldn't help it. The seriousness of the situation was really coming home to her now.

'Grace, are you okay?' The voice came from behind her. Donovan had leaned forward, his head almost resting on her shoulder. The concern on his face made her catch her breath.

If she had to be exposed to something nasty, at least she had one of the best in her corner. No matter what he looked like, as a doctor he was brilliant.

She was in safe hands. Figuratively and literally.

'Turn around,' she said briskly to him. He snapped to attention, meeting her glare. There was no point in trying to pretend he hadn't been staring.

'What?'

She spun her index figures in circles. 'Turn around, so I can do *your* back.' Of course. She'd spoken to him as if he was an idiot. Which at this point he was.

Her eyes were fixed firmly on his. He could almost see the determination in her glare that she wouldn't make the same mistake he just had and look in places she shouldn't. That sent an immediate rush of blood through his system and he pivoted on his heels quickly.

No. This was work. This was an emergency situation. His body might be reacting with a rush of hormones but his brain wouldn't let him go there.

Her hands scrubbed his back a little more roughly than required. He so wanted to lighten the moment, so wanted to quip, *Wanna go lower?* But Grace Barclay wouldn't find it funny.

He started scrubbing his face to try and take his mind off the fact there was a very gorgeous, very curvaceous, naked brunette inches away from him. All his fantasies about a woman in the shower with him hadn't started like this.

What could they just have been exposed to?

His brain flooded with possibilities. Anthrax, botulism, cholera, smallpox, bubonic plague. The list was pretty long. All high-priority agents that could be used in a bioterrorism attack. Easily spread and transmitted from person to person, with high death rates and the potential for spreading panic.

Some of his colleagues called him Worst-Case Don. And it was true. He always imagined the worst-case scenario in any situation. It was his mantra. *Plan for the worst, hope for the best*. It was what any doctor working at the DPA should do.

He looked back over to the wall. Steam was clouding the clock's face so he strode across the tiled floor and wiped it clean with a towel.

'Time's up, Grace,' he called, reaching for the switch to the showers. But she hadn't heard. The showers around here didn't halt automatically. No, they had some weird anomaly that meant for the final few seconds they turned icy cold. Everyone around here knew about it.

Half the fun of new recruits was letting them find out for themselves.

He picked up a towel and started rough-drying his legs, smiling as he heard the yelp behind him.

'Yaoow!'

There was the padding of wet feet behind him and the noise of someone whipping a towel from the top of the pile on the bench.

'You did that deliberately!'

He looked over his shoulder, vaguely aware that right now Grace Barclay had a prime time view of his bare backside. 'I did not. I shouted to warn you. You obviously didn't hear above the noise from the showers.'

'Obviously.' The word dripped with sarcasm.

He wrapped a towel around his waist. The immediate crisis was over; it was time to start handling a whole new one. He turned to face her.

Grace was holding the towel directly in front of her bare body. She hadn't even had time to wrap it around herself. If someone came in the door behind her they would get an unholy view of Grace Barclay.

He pointed to the scrubs in the corner. 'Get dressed. Someone should be along to let us know if the isolation room is ready.'

He pulled a set of navy scrubs over his head. Already the room seemed too small. Donovan didn't do well in small spaces. Maybe it was the steam? Clouding his vision and taking up space. If the air-con had been working, this would have been gone in seconds.

There was a knock at the door. Through the glass he could see the outline of a hazmat suit. A face appeared at the door.

He breathed a sigh of relief. Frank, from the lab. He already spent most of his day in one of these suits. They'd probably just unplugged him, fastened him to an oxygen cylinder and sent him upstairs.

He signalled a thumbs-up. 'Ready, Grace?' She'd wound her hair in a wet knot at the nape of her neck and was wearing a pale green set of scrubs.

There. That was better. That was the sight he was used to—a colleague in a set of scrubs. Now he didn't need to worry about his eyes wandering to places they shouldn't.

She gave the slightest of nods. He paused for a second. He might be known as a brilliant doctor with an encyclopaedic knowledge, but his people skills were sometimes lacking. Should he have sat her down and given her a pep talk? She looked a little pale. Her hand was pressed against the wall as if to stop her body swaying.

But there was no time for pep talks. Donovan needed to be surrounded by colleagues who conducted themselves in a professional manner. There were things to do. Tests to be ordered. Clean-up precautions to be taken. Risk assessments made on the exposure of others. Chances were he'd be stuck in an isolation room with Grace for hours—maybe days. There'd be plenty of time for pep talks later.

Her gaze met his. 'Let's go.' Was she trying to convince herself or him?

He didn't really have time to think about it, and if Grace Barclay was a potential member of his team she was going to have to be ready for anything.

He pulled open the door and gestured towards spacesuited Frank. 'Then let's go.'

Ninety minutes later Grace had been X-rayed and her bloods were being analysed in the lab. She was still in shock.

The negative pressure room was used frequently for training scenarios at the DPA. She'd been in it countless times—she'd just never expected to be a patient in one.

The glass walls reached from ceiling to floor, leaving every aspect of them on view to outside observers. The only part of the room that had any modicum of privacy was the screened-off bathroom and shower area. In the meantime, she and Donovan were prime viewing material to the rest of the department, who all seemed to be staring at them from outside.

People were scurrying around, huddled in conversations, talking on phones. All busy. All doing their jobs. Grace just wished she could be out there with them.

It was like being a goldfish in a bowl. A big bowl, with a shark circling inside.

Donovan didn't seem to like being in isolation either. He hadn't stopped talking since he'd got in here—talking about everything and anything. If she didn't know better she'd have thought he was nervous or a bit agitated. But that didn't fit with what she knew about Donovan Reid. The guy was practically a legend around here.

Last year he'd led work on an outbreak of West Nile virus, saving the lives of over a hundred people because of his rapid diagnostic skills. Then there had been the incident that had made the news the year before. Donovan had shown complete and utter self-control when dealing with a gunman who'd entered a hospital where the DPA was working. He'd managed to persuade the gunman to release some hostages and had eventually tackled and disarmed the guy himself. Donovan Reid was every schoolgirl's hero. But it wasn't helping her head. She pressed her fingers to her temples and started rotating them in small circles.

'Has Frank been able to isolate anything in the lab yet? What about the blood tests? Have they shown anything? Is Bill Cutler from the FBI here yet?'

Grace swung her legs up onto one of the two beds in the room and leaned back against the pillows. Her wet hair was really beginning to annoy her. She'd never be able to sleep. She closed her eyes for a second. 'Donovan, any chance of some quiet? I have a killer headache.' The words were out before she'd even thought about them.

'What?' He spun around, his forehead creased with lines. He crossed the room in a few strides, putting his hand on her head.

A prickling sensation swept over her skin. The expression on his face was serious. Maybe this wasn't the start of a migraine. Could this be a symptom of something? She hadn't even considered that.

But she didn't need to. Because Donovan was considering it all for her. Out loud. 'When did your headache start? Is this normal for you? How is your vision—are you having any problems?'

She reached her hand up and put it over his, squeezing her eyes closed and trying to ignore the instant tingle that shot up her arm like a pulse.

Just like when he'd touched her in the shower.

Could this day get any worse?

She swallowed. Her mouth was dry, she was desperate for something to drink. Was there even water in this fishbowl?

She removed Donovan's hand from her head.

'Stop it. You're not helping. I suffer from migraines but I haven't had one for the last four years.' She didn't even want to open her eyes, the spotlights around them were just too bright.

He sighed with relief. 'Thank goodness. What can I do to help?'

'Stop talking?' She squinted out the corner of one eye.

He smiled. The first time he'd smiled since they'd got in the isolation room.

'Never gonna happen.'

Her stomach rumbled loudly and she pressed her hands over it in embarrassment.

'Would some food help? Or some meds?'

She nodded. Having a migraine around Dr Handsome was bad enough. Having it under the spotlight of just around every member of staff was even worse.

She mumbled the name of the meds she normally used. The normally brisk manner he used around others had vanished. 'Can you put the lights down?' she asked.

He hesitated for a second. 'Sure, I'll keep you under my watchful eye.' He walked over to the wall. Every word they said in here, every noise they made could be heard by the outside world.

'Can we get some migraine meds for Grace, please? And can someone put the lights down around here?'

There were a few nods and some words exchanged by members of staff. Anna walked over to the glass. 'Grace, are your meds in your locker? I can get them from your bag.'

Grace nodded. Donovan was back at her side. 'What do you want to eat? We need to plan on being in here for the next few hours—maybe even the next few days.' He gave her a cheeky grin. 'We can order in—what's your favourite?'

She laughed and shook her head. 'You're joking, right?'

'Why?' He held up his hands. 'Anything that comes into this room goes through the cross-contamination system. We can ask for anything. It's only our air that can't get out.' He raised his eyebrows, 'Personally, I'm going to order a pepperoni pizza and a pastrami on rye for later.'

She smiled as her stomach growled again.

'Well, there is something that helps my migraines.'

'What?'

She named a coffee house a few minutes away from the DPA. 'I've used it for years. They have the best skinny sugar-free caramel lattes and banana and toffee muffins I've ever tasted.'

He frowned, as if his brain was trying to process her female logic. 'The skinny latte counteracts the banana and toffee muffin?'

She grinned. 'Exactly. You get it. It's all about the calories, Donovan.' She pointed at his washboard stomach. 'Though I'm sure you'd spontaneously combust if you ate anything like that. You probably don't even know what a banana muffin looks like.'

He leaned forward and lowered his voice, just as the lights flickered off around them. His eyebrows arched as a dim glow of pale blue appeared, giving their skin a strange pallor. 'It's only work-related things that make me spontaneously combust, Grace. I can assure you I'm well acquainted with the muffin family.' He gave her a wicked smile. 'And from where I was standing you certainly don't need to worry about calories.'

She felt her cheeks burn. How would they look in this strange light? Had she just imagined it, or had Donovan Reid just given her a backhanded compliment?

There was no hiding her curves. She was never going to look like one of the gym bunnies he normally dated. But maybe that wasn't his preference.

There hadn't been time to think earlier. No time to be shy. He'd seen every single part of her—scars and all.

The thought of his fingers brushing over her shoulder scar sent shivers down her spine. He must have noticed it, but he certainly hadn't mentioned it.

He'd seen her ample breasts, rounded stomach and curved hips and thighs. Her backside didn't even feature in her thoughts. In her head it was her best feature—round enough to rival J-Lo's. If only she had J-Lo's matching height…

There was a hiss of air, doors were opening, items left to be decompressed before the second set of doors opened. Her migraine tablets were pressed into her hands, along with a glass of water, and she swallowed them gratefully.

Donovan Reid had never struck her as the kind of man to have a good bedside manner. He wasn't much of a people person—his mind was always focused on the job. He'd been the youngest team leader around here for the last four years.

And the last few years had been tough. A potential outbreak of smallpox, discovered by an ex-employee, followed by one of the biggest operations the DPA had ever been involved in. Donovan had missed that call by a matter of minutes. She could only imagine how much he'd smarted about that.

And now another member of his team was pregnant. Jokes had been circulating the office for the last year about a certain swivel chair. Callie Sawyer, Violet Hunter and now Mhairi Spencer had all sat in that chair at some point. Grace and her friends had vowed not to sit in it for the next five years.

She swallowed her tablets and sighed, leaning back against the pillows. They were softer than she'd thought; she could almost forget about her still damp hair. If she closed her eyes just for a minute, she might feel a little better. She sank down into the comfort zone, tugging the soft blanket up around her shoulders. She could day-dream for a few seconds.

Daydream about what she really would have liked to have happened in that shower. Donovan to give her a cheeky wink and sexy smile, loving her curves and having a look of pure lust in his eyes for her. Donovan, with his light brown curls, chiselled jaw and sculpted body. For her eyes only. Ah, well, a girl could dream.

She could hear mumbling. Donovan was in deep talks through the glass with Frank. He gave a sigh and walked over to her.

She sat up. 'What is it?'

'Oh, good. You're awake.'

She rubbed her eyes and looked around. 'Was I sleeping?'

He nodded. 'Just for the last thirty minutes.'

Great. In the middle of a crisis with the man she wanted to impress and she'd fallen asleep. 'What have I missed? Has something happened?'

'Yes, well, no. It's good,' actually. Frank couldn't screen the sample until it had been irradiated. At first glance it's not anthrax and it's not any form of plague.'

She let out the breath she hadn't even realised shed been holding. 'Well, that's good, isn't it? Maybe it's something stupid. Maybe it's flour or talcum powder—something like that? Something that means we'll be okay.'

He ran his fingers through his already mussed-up hair. 'It'll take a few hours before we know anything for sure.'

She could read in his eyes exactly how he felt about that, he was watching everyone outside rush around. 'And you can't stand the thought of being stuck in here? You're wandering about like a caged animal. Don't you know the meaning of the word "chill"?'

As soon as the words were out of her mouth she knew she'd made a big mistake. He whipped around to face her, his eyes as black as coal. His expression matched.

'How can I chill, Grace? The DPA has just received a potential biological hazard through the mail system. No note. No explanation Nothing. Just an Arkansas postmark. Hundreds of people in our department could have been exposed. Hundreds of mail workers could have come into contact with that letter. If this *is* a biological contagion, this could be a disaster. And you want me to chill? This is my watch, Grace, these people are my responsibility.'

She gulped. Oh, no. She'd just killed any chance of impressing Donovan Reid. He probably thought she was a dumb-ass schoolkid. All thoughts of powerful thighs and six-packs were flying out of the window, although she reserved the right to conjure them back up in her dreams. She stammered, 'A-and it's m-my f-fault—because I opened the package?'

His eyes widened. 'Is that what you think? Why on earth would I blame you, Grace? You only did what anyone would do—you opened the envelope.'

She held out her hands. Her migraine really wasn't improving. The thirty-minute nap hadn't helped. The meds hadn't even touched the edge of her pain. 'But look at the effect it's had on the whole department.'

He shook his head. 'Don't read too much into my ranting, Grace. I hate that I can't be out there, doing more. It doesn't matter who opened that envelope today, the effect was always going to be the same.'

He moved over next to her and lifted an electronic BP cuff from the wall, switching on the monitor with his thumb.

'What are you doing?'

'Your migraine isn't any better, is it?'

She shook her head as he wrapped the cuff around her arm. 'I'm doing what any good doctor should. I'm checking your BP. Maybe it's not a migraine. Maybe it's something else entirely.'

Her stomach gave a little flip. Back to the whole 'you've breathed in a contagion and are going to die' scenario. She was trying to keep that one from her head right now. If this was a tension headache it was only going to get a whole lot worse.

She felt the cuff inflate, cutting off the circulation to her arm. These darned things always felt as if they overinflated and any minute now her fingers would fall off. After what seemed like for ever it gave a gentle hiss and started to go down.

Donovan's eyes stayed on the monitor, watching the figures. He leaned over and pulled the cuff free. 'Perfect. Your blood pressure is fine.'

A few minutes later the food appeared and was placed in the decompression section between the doors. After the obligatory number of minutes the second set of doors hissed open and smell of pepperoni pizza and caramel latte wafted into the room.

Their stomachs grumbled in unison and they both laughed. Donovan opened the pizza box and grabbed a slice. 'Mmm, delicious. I hadn't got round to having lunch earlier. I was just about to eat at my desk when someone…' he gave her the eye '…decided to brighten up my day.'

She should be feeling guilty that she'd managed to eat some of her sandwich while Donovan Reid had worked out at the gym. But as his muscled body had proved too much of a distraction, most of her sandwich had ended up in the trash. And the smell surrounding her was just what she needed.

Grace took a long sip of her latte, letting the smooth, sweet caramel hit the spot. It was just the perfect temperature. Someone had obviously had to spend ten minutes walking it back from the coffee house. She took a bite of the muffin. Perfect. 'Fabulous. I love these. I could eat them all day.'

'Wouldn't you get sick of them?' He was watching her. As if he was curious about her.

'Are you crazy? Of course I wouldn't. I limit myself to one a week because there's about a billion calories in each one.' She licked some toffee from her finger. 'But you know what? I love every single one of them.'

He was watching her appreciatively. Apart from being naked in the shower, it was the first time she'd noticed him run his eyes up and down her body, although right now he was focused entirely on her fingers. She tried not to smile.

It hadn't even crossed her mind that her actions could seem provocative. She'd been too busy enjoying her muffin. But somehow the thought of

Donovan Reid having those kinds of thoughts about her was sending shivers down her spine. He'd never even noticed her before. He hadn't even known her name.

Her gaze met his and he looked away hurriedly. But not before she'd caught the expression in his eyes. One of pure lust. Wow.

He glanced at his watch, cursed and pulled his phone out of his pocket.

'What's wrong?' She looked over at the clock. It was just after six. Chances were they would be stuck in here all night. Was Dr Handsome going to have to break a date?

He took a couple of steps away from her—as if that made any difference in an isolation room. There was no privacy in here.

His voice was deliberately low as he left a message on a machine, 'Hi, Hannah, sorry I couldn't catch you. I've got a problem at work. I could be here a while. Possibly even overnight.'

She could almost imagine the lithe blonde model of the moment weeping into the salad she was about to miss at her cancelled dinner date. But then things took a strange turn.

'So, if you don't mind, could you check on Casey for me? Do what needs to be done? You've got the keys to my apartment. Thanks. I'll be in touch.'

Now Grace was confused. That hadn't seemed like a broken dinner date. 'Who's Casey?' The words were out before she could stop them. Being confined with Donovan Reid was giving her a confidence that had been missing for a long time.

He shot her a look. Would he tell her it was none of her business? No, he was scrolling through something on his phone. He turned it around. 'Casey's my dog. He's a bit old and temperamental.'

'Wonder where he gets that from?' She leaned forward to look at the photo, which had obviously been snapped in a park somewhere, of a black and white terrier-type dog. She looked at Donovan and wrinkled her nose. 'I didn't take you for a dog person.'

'Really? Why not?' Was he offended?

She shrugged. 'You're too intense. Always totally focused on the job. I always imagined you live in one of those sparkling white apartments that you're hardly ever in. A dog's a commitment. You just didn't strike me as a commitment sort of guy.'

He folded him arms across his chest and looked amused. 'Well, there's a character assassination if I've ever heard one.'

'What?' Her heart beat started to quicken. 'No, I didn't mean it like that.'

'Yes, you did. And that's what I like about you, Grace Barclay, you say what's on your mind. You don't spend six hours trying to think of how to word it.'

She let out a little laugh. 'Okay, guilty as charged. I sometimes speak without thinking.' She shook her head. 'But I'd never, ever deliberately offend someone.' She raised her chin, 'I happen to think Casey looks like a great little character.'

Donovan wagged his finger at her, 'Oh, no, don't ever let him hear you call him little.'

'He won't like it?'

'He definitely won't like it.' The atmosphere between them was changing. It was almost as if he was *flirting* with her. Did Donovan Reid even do that? Maybe she *was* under the effect of some weird disease and it was playing havoc with her brain cells.

'Will your dogsitter be able to help out?'

He gave a brief nod. 'Always. Hannah's very reliable. She'll go around as soon as she gets the message and make sure Casey's walked, fed and watered.'

Her imagination immediately started whipping up pictures of what Hannah looked like. A woman with a key to Donovan's apartment? But something distracted her. There was a huddle of people outside the glass. But she was far more interested in the conversation that seemed to be happening outside. Six of her colleagues were gesticulating and arguing about something.

'Donovan…' She pointed her finger. Her heart sank. Please don't let them have discovered it was some weird, deadly disease. They were obviously drawing lots to see who would tell them.

Donovan looked over his shoulder and his gaze narrowed. 'What's going on?' He strode over to the glass. 'Has something happened?'

There were a few mumbles, before one of the

staff members was finally selected to answer the question. He walked over and spoke in a low tone to Donovan. Questions were fired backwards and forwards.

After a few seconds Donovan turned to face her. But it wasn't fear on his face. His brow was furrowed and the tiny lines around his blue eyes had deepened. It was total confusion. He ran his fingers through his hair and shook his head as he took a few steps towards her, 'Grace, what do you know about the Marburg virus?'

CHAPTER TWO

WOW. TOTALLY OUT of left field. So *not* what she had been expecting him to say.

It took a few seconds for her scrambled brain to get itself in order. Then her professional mode switched into play. Donovan Reid wasn't the only one around here with an encyclopaedic knowledge—she just hadn't had much opportunity to show hers off.

She swung her legs off the bed and walked towards him. 'What's going on? The Marburg virus? Is that what we've got?' Because from what she could remember, she certainly wouldn't want to have it.

He shook his head. 'No. It's not what we've got. But someone else has it—down in Florida. First case in the US in years.' He started pacing around; she could tell he was agitated. Desperate to get out of this glass box and start dealing with another infectious disease. Donovan Reid was permanently looking for the next disaster to deal with. And this would be the biggest disaster since the suspected smallpox outbreak. How on earth could an African disease be in the US?

She screwed up her face. The migraine was still there, but the dimmed blue lights were definitely helping—as was the fact she'd had something to eat. Along with the meds and the quick thirty-minute nap she might actually shake this off.

The blue glow was doing strange things to Donovan Reid's skin. It was almost like being in a nightclub. She didn't even want to think how pale it was currently making her look.

She reeled off the first thing that came into her head. 'Marburg haemorrhagic fever. First discovered in Germany in the 1960s where workers were exposed to infected tissues from monkeys. Now it's usually passed to humans by bats. Previous cases have mainly been in Africa, or in travellers who'd just visited. There's no vaccine, no real cure, just treatment of symptoms.'

Donovan spun around to face her, his eyebrows

lifting appreciatively. 'Well, well, I'm impressed. All that with no computer in front of you.'

She folded her arms across her chest. This was it. This was her chance. A chance to make up for her earlier blunder and try and find a foothold into his team.

Everyone wanted to get a permanent place on one of the fieldwork teams. It was the cutting edge of disease detective work. The front line in dealing with patients and making the biggest difference to the prevention of infectious disease.

She'd made an agreement with girls earlier to fight dirty for a place on his team. It was time to show him just how encyclopaedic her brain was.

'Actually, that's the just the summary. Would you like me to tell you the rest of the details? The fact that the last known case was in Uganda? It's got an incubation period of five to ten days. And it's got between a twenty-three to ninety per cent fatality rate.'

Oh, yeah. She was batting big style now. Being trapped in here hadn't been much fun. Getting naked in front of Donovan Reid had been nothing short of humiliating.

There had to be at least one bonus in this lousy day.

Her mouth was running away with her now. 'Under the microscope it has a really distinctive shape—like a shepherd's crook, which means it's rarely mistaken for anything else.'

She saw the flicker of amusement in his blue eyes. 'That's okay, Grace, that's more than enough.'

Just as well. The light in here was doing distracting things to his blue eyes. Enhancing the colour and making them look a movie-star bright shade of blue. She was fast losing all concentration.

David, one of the other doctors, was reading a whole host of information through the glass to Donovan about the lab tests. 'Frank just got phoned about these. He's confirming the results.'

It was standard procedure. Most labs weren't equipped to do the specialist tests that the DPA carried out. Anomalies were noted, along with patient's symptoms and if there was any query of infectious disease, the samples were forwarded to the DPA.

'Do we know anything about the victim?'

Victim. Not patient. It only meant one thing.

'They're dead?'

David nodded. 'They died an hour ago. But they've had a child admitted with similar symptoms, so we've got a rush on to try and get a diagnosis.'

It made sense. Once they had a diagnosis they could find the best possible treatment for the patient.

David was still reading from the paper in his hand. 'Jessie Tanner, sixty-seven, from Florida. Admitted four days ago with diarrhoea, vomiting, maculopapular rash and jaundice.'

That name.

Grace's skin prickled, every hair on her arms standing on end. There was no air movement in the isolation room but she could almost swear a cold breeze had just blasted her. No. It couldn't be. It just couldn't.

David was still talking, 'Deteriorated rapidly. Didn't respond to IV or oxygen support.'

'Oh, no.' Her hand covered her mouth. She was trying frantically to remember. When was the last time she'd spoken to her? Had she said anything different? 'Oh, no. I've missed something. I didn't take her seriously.'

Donovan frowned. 'What on earth are you talking about. Grace? How on earth would you know someone in Florida?' His face paled, 'Is it family?' There was an edge to his voice, a real concern.

Grace shook her head fiercely, her heart beating furiously in her chest. 'You don't get it, Donovan. It's her. Jessie Tanner phones here every day.'

'What for?' He didn't get it. It was clear he had no idea what she was talking about.

She took a deep breath, 'Donovan, Jessie Tanner is crazy bat lady.'

'What?' All the heads outside the isolation room shot round at the rise in pitch in Donovan's voice.

Grace jerked back as if she'd just been stung by a wasp.

He couldn't believe his ears. This wasn't happening. It just wasn't. This was one of those crazy, muddled dreams you had, with totally random things happening all around.

Nothing about today seemed real.

Least of all being naked in a shower with Grace.

He put his hand on her shoulder, trying to make sense of what she'd just said. 'How can you be sure?' He had a bad feeling about this.

She took a deep breath. 'Because I remember things. I remember details. That's her name. That's where she lives.' Grace put her head in her hands and groaned. 'She hasn't phoned the last few days. I wondered what was wrong with her.'

Donovan looked at David. 'Get the call log. Find out the last time she called and who spoke to her. Find out what her query was.' David walked away swiftly.

Grace lifted her hands. 'But it's the same thing every day. It's always questions about the bats. There are some in the caves near her, and in the forest next to her.'

She screwed up her face. 'But how could African fruit bats get to a cave in Florida?'

David shook his head. 'African fruit bats probably couldn't, but Jamaican fruit bats could. I'll get someone from environmental health or the fish and wildlife service.'

There was a movement to their side. Frank from the lab. This time he wasn't wearing the hazmat suit and he had something in his hands. He pushed the button outside the isolation room's pressurised doors, not waiting for the second set to close before he walked in.

He was laughing, holding up the sample bottle with a tiny bit of powder in the bottom.

Donovan caught the shout in his throat. Frank had been here longer than him. He knew more about biohazards than Donovan ever would. It must be safe. *They* must be safe.

'What is it?'

Frank smiled, he was shaking his head. 'You'll never believe it.'

'Try me.' He wasn't in the mood for jokes. The sooner he knew that the staff around him hadn't been exposed to anything dangerous the better.

'It's honey dust.'

'What?' Of all the things in the world he'd

expected to hear, that hadn't featured at all. No wonder Grace's skin and hair had glistened.

Frank kept laughing. 'I know. I can't believe it either. Must have been some high-school kids playing a prank.'

Now he knew his staff were safe Donovan felt his blood pressure rising. 'Some prank. They shut down our agency for the last few hours.' He waved his hands around the isolation room. 'Look at the procedures we had to put in place. I don't even want to guess how much this has cost us.'

Frank shrugged. 'I'm just glad we don't have a full-scale incident on our hands. This could have been our worst nightmare.' He lifted his hands. 'I'll take a high-school prank over a real-life disaster any day.'

'What's honey dust?' Her voice was quiet, timid. He'd almost forgotten she was standing behind him.

He and Frank exchanged a glance. Grace Barclay didn't know what honey dust was. Who was going to tell her?

Frank pressed the sample bottle into Donovan's

hand with a glint in his eye. 'I'll leave this with you, Don. I've let the lead investigator from the FBI know we'll be standing down. I take it they'll fingerprint the letter and try and track it.' He was still smiling, his gaze flicking back towards Grace. 'I have some more tests to run on another possible outbreak. Come and see me in an hour.'

The Marburg virus. He'd need to deal with that as soon as possible.

Frank left, chuckling away to himself as Grace continued to stare at Donovan.

She stepped towards him, fixing her green eyes on his. 'I don't get it. What's going on? What's honey dust? I take it's not dangerous?'

He shook his head and tried to hide his smile. 'Dangerous—no.'

'And?'

There was no way out of this. He was just going to have to spell it out. 'It's a type of body powder, it makes the skin glow and…it tastes like honey.'

'Why on earth would it taste like—? Oh.' Her eyes widened as realisation struck home. Her cheeks flushed with colour and she instantly looked down at the floor. 'Someone sent that as a prank? Wow.'

She was embarrassed. And he liked it. Her feet shuffled nervously on the floor, her hand twiddling a still-damp strand of her hair.

He really ought to put her out of her misery and change the conversation, but this was kind of cute.

The more he was around her, the more she piqued his curiosity. He rubbed his finger and thumb together. He could almost still feel the smoothness of her skin, along with the angry, ragged stab wound. There was more to Grace Barclay than met the eye.

He cleared his throat. 'We'll need to do a debrief about this later. The Director will expect one.' He looked around him, 'We've only ever done drills in here before. This time we had a real life chance to see how things could work out.' He picked up some notes that he'd scribbled earlier. 'Maybe this wasn't such a bad thing after all. I can think of a few areas for improvement. How about you?'

She sighed and leaned against the glass wall.

'I don't ever want to be in here again—drill or no drill.'

He smiled. He knew exactly how she felt. 'Me neither. I'm sort of hoping that my suit and shoes haven't already been incinerated.'

She cringed. 'I'd forgotten about that. Darn it. That was my favourite shirt.'

'Mine too. It brings out the colour of your eyes.'

Their gazes locked together for a second, ignoring the movements around them as the news spread and their colleagues realised the crisis had ended.

He'd meant it. And the words had come out before he'd had a chance to think about them. Being in close quarters with someone did that to you. Made you say things you really shouldn't.

She shot him a sarcastic smile, 'Yeah, right, Donovan. This from the guy who a few hours ago didn't even know my name.'

He shrugged. 'I know you lunch every Friday in the staffroom opposite the gym.'

Her mouth gaped a little. Did she really think he hadn't noticed her? His cool act was working way better than he thought.

Grace Barclay was smart. She'd been able to tell him about Marburg virus off the top of her head. She'd connected the dots and realised who Jessie Tanner was. It could have taken them days to find that connection. She was gorgeous. And had a body to die for.

What more could a man want?

His focus shifted. He could think about the last few hours later. Right now he had another priority—one in which it seemed the DPA was already implicated.

'How do you feel about fieldwork, Grace?'

She shuffled her feet. It seemed to be her 'thing'. The trait that revealed her nerves. But the gaze she met his with was steady. She was doing her best to give the impression of someone with confidence.

'I'd really like to get some experience. I've been here for the last seven months. Apart from a few practical assignments with Callum Ferguson, I've not had much experience.'

Callum Ferguson, the longest-serving member of the DPA. They even called him the Granddad of Disease. If she'd done a few practical assignments with Callum then she'd learned from the master. He hadn't heard anyone complain about her.

It secured the thoughts he'd already been toying with. He had a vacancy in his team that needed to be filled. In everyday circumstances he'd ask for all the files of his junior colleagues and look for a suitable replacement. He'd ask around for recommendations—find out who was ready for the next step.

But he didn't need to do that now. And he didn't want to waste time. If Marburg virus was the next big outbreak he wanted a full team available to investigate.

They were free now. Free to get out of this isolation room and get back to work. And he knew exactly who he wanted to work with.

He held out his hand towards her. 'Grace Barclay, welcome to the team.'

CHAPTER THREE

GRACE WAS FROZEN. She wanted to jump up and down and let out a scream. But professionalism stopped her.

Instead, she reached out her hand to take Donovan's. Zing. The current shot straight up her arm. She couldn't acknowledge it. She was watching his eyes for any hint that he might have felt it too. But Donovan Reid was as cool as the proverbial cucumber.

'Are you sure? You don't need to do an interview or an evaluation?'

He shook his head. 'My team. My choice. I'd only need to go to internal interviews if I didn't have a candidate.' He gave her a smile. 'But I do. Do you want to be part of the team, Grace?'

Did she want to be part of the team? Did teenage girls dream of being Mrs Beiber? Did every medical student dream of meeting their own Dr McDreamy or McSteamy?

She shot him her best beaming smile. 'I'd love to be part of the team, Donovan. What do you want me to do first?'

'Why didn't I open the envelope?' groaned Anna as she flopped down on Grace's bed.

Lara was much more pragmatic as she poured wine into three glasses. 'Well, even if I had opened the envelope, I would never have remembered all the stuff about Marburg virus off the top of my head.' She raised her glass, 'So, here's to you, Grace. The best girl won.'

Grace's stomach gave a little flip as she reached for her glass and clinked it against her friends'. She knew they were happy for her, even though there was deep-rooted envy. It was normal in their profession. They all wanted to do their best.

Lara walked over to her wardrobe and started pulling out clothes. 'Yes, yes, no, no, definitely no.' Clothes were littered over the room like coloured fluttering butterflies.

'What do you think you're doing?'

'We're helping you pack. You're going to Florida with the best-looking guy for miles around. I want to make sure you look your best.'

She held up a bright orange bikini. 'Oh, yes!'

'Oh, no.' Grace grabbed it from the bed and stuffed it in a drawer. 'I won't have cause to wear a bikini. It's the last thing I'll need.' She looked at the other things on the bed, picking up one of her black skirts. 'What's wrong with this? Why did it get a no?'

Anna giggled. 'I can tell you. It's too old-fashioned. It doesn't enhance your best bits.'

'And what are they, if I have them?'

She rolled her eyes and picked up an alternative, pencil skirt. 'Your ass!' both girls said in unison.

Lara pulled out a couple of dresses and fitted shirts. 'These are the same style, pencil skirts that show off your shape and fitted dresses that make us all jealous of your boobs.'

She wrinkled her nose at the bright blue dress and similar styled black and white polka-dot one. 'Aren't they a bit *too* fitted for work? I'm not sure that's what I should be wearing.'

Anna shook her head and held one up. 'What's wrong? They cover all the bits that should be covered, they're a perfectly respectable length and—look—no sleeves. It's going to be hot down in Florida. You need to be comfortable.'

Lara nodded, holding up a red and then a bright pink shirt. 'And these will look great with your black pencil skirt. You need to wear more colour, Grace. It suits you.'

'Why do I feel as if you're giving me a secret makeover?'

Anna and Lara exchanged knowing glances, before sitting on either side of her on the bed. Lara tapped her thigh. 'We just don't want you to waste a valuable opportunity.'

Anna had started lifting her hair and was looking at it as if she was imagining taking a pair of scissors to it. 'Stop that!' Grace batted her hand away. 'My valuable opportunity is my chance to prove myself as a capable fieldwork team member.' Maybe if she kept saying it loudly enough she might start believing it herself.

The thought of being stuck on a flight between Atlanta and Northwest Florida Beaches with

Donovan Reid was more than a little daunting. Now the crisis was over and a new investigation was starting, she was sure he would have lost all interest in her.

Maybe rethinking her wardrobe wasn't such a bad idea at all?

Lara tapped her shoulder and dumped a set of straighteners in her suitcase. 'Watch out for the frizz down there, it's very humid.' She lifted a strand of Grace's hair too. 'You should maybe think about a deep conditioning treatment.'

Grace stood up, 'What is the obsession with my hair? Is something wrong with it?'

She stood in front of the mirror looking at her reflection. She'd had long brown hair for as long as she could remember. On the odd occasion she might get some highlights or the odd hair dye job when she got it trimmed, but apart from that she usually tied it up for work. She frowned, taking a look at her ends. Maybe it was a bit straggly. Maybe it could do with a tidy up?

'Do you think I should get it cut?'

Anna stood behind her, putting her hands around either shoulder and resting them on her shoulder bones. 'What about a few inches? It might be easier to handle. Give it a bit more volume.'

Grace took a deep breath. She'd never had her hair that short before. She looked at the several straggly inches that hung beneath the position of Anna's hands. Maybe it wasn't such a bad idea.

She looked at the clock. 'I don't have time. I need to be at the airport in five hours. I'll never be able to get my hair cut before then.'

Lara swung her legs off the bed. 'Yes, you can. There's a salon in the mall that stays open really late. I'll call them now.'

'But what about my packing?'

Anna shrugged. 'I'll do it. Look out some toiletries and some underwear. I'll just throw in everything we've got on the bed, along with shoes and some casual gear for under the hazmat suit.'

She'd forgotten about that. Wearing the hazmat suits in a hot climate was going to be really uncomfortable. Thank goodness her friends could keep her right.

She looked at the clothes on the bed. Truth was, if her friends left right now, she'd probably pack a whole load of bland clothes that she wouldn't even think about. Having their expertise was actually quite exciting after all, Donovan had commented how much he liked her green shirt…

'Come on, slowcoach!' yelled Lara. 'I've just spoken to the salon. They can take you in twenty minutes. Let's go.'

Grace grabbed her bag. A new haircut. A re-vamped wardrobe. And a chance to prove herself to her team leader. What more could a girl want?

Donovan stuffed things into his carryon bag. He hated luggage with a passion and had no intention of standing around while a conveyer belt of multicoloured suitcases filed past at two miles per hour. He only hoped the rest of team were as prepared as he was.

He folded one suit and a couple of shirts and ties. The rest of his clothes were casual. He was going to be on the ground investigating or in the local lab. He wouldn't need a lot of professional clothes. Just as well, as his latest suit and handmade shoes had just been incinerated. He winced when he remembered how much those shoes had cost. It had seemed like such a good idea at the time—spend a little extra, shoes that were measured and moulded to fit. It had been like wearing a pair of comfortable slippers, the Italian leather had been so pliable. Too bad they were gone for ever.

He flung his shaving gear and toiletries into a wash bag and stuffed that inside his bag. His last item was his most essential. His tablet. He'd stored all the information that the DPA had on Marburg virus, along with incidences and procedures manuals. He liked to have everything he needed at the touch of a button.

He smiled. Or maybe he should just have Grace Barclay at his side. Her knowledge seemed to rival his own and he liked it. He liked it a lot.

He glanced around his apartment. White, clean lines everywhere. She'd pretty much nailed the place with her description. Not that it bothered him. He wasn't fixated on soft furnishings and curtains. He was much more interested in the glass around him. The view of open space.

As long as he had a window with a view outdoors he was fine. Put him in a room with no windows and within a few minutes he started to get antsy. It wasn't a big deal. Because he didn't let it be. He'd never used the elevators at the DPA. The stairs were the healthier option anyway, and there were windows in the stairwell. It didn't matter that they were small, they were still there. And that's what was important.

Up until now the only place in the DPA that had really made him uncomfortable was Frank's lab. A totally enclosed environment. It needed to be. There were too many potential toxins in that lab. Any of them escaping into the natural environment would be a disaster.

He'd just about held it together today in the isolation room. There had been lots of practice drills involving the room before but he'd always had a timescale. He'd always known he'd only be in there for a few hours. Today the timescale had been indeterminable, and it had almost given him away.

At one point he'd noticed Grace's green eyes fixed on him, watching the slight tremor in his hands with a question in her eyes. He'd ignored them. Had focused on one of the many other things that he'd had to be concerned about. It had helped. It had helped him stop visualising the walls of the elevator he'd been trapped in as a child. Six long hours in an elevator by himself. It had seemed like fun for a six-year-old to jump in the elevator and press the button, watching the doors slide closed on his horrified mother's face. Typical mischievous little-boy behaviour. Only it hadn't been so much fun when the lift had ground to a halt.

It hadn't been fun at all when the alarm hadn't sounded when he'd pressed the button and it had felt as if no one could hear him shout.

It had taken him a long time to finally hear the distant voices of adults calling to him.

Six hours, staring at four walls, was a long, lonely time for a little boy. It had felt like for ever. His imagination had run riot and left him with a permanent, and no doubt irrational, fear of being trapped again.

So windows were his friends. If he could see out of a window he was fine. Anything else he kept brief and to the point. Enclosed spaces were definitely time limited for Donovan Reid.

There was a nuzzle of something wet and soft at his feet. Casey. He bent down and picked up the little terrier, giving him a hug. 'Hey, boy. You're getting collected any time. You're going to stay with Auntie Hannah for a few days.' He was lucky. Not only did Hannah dog-walk for him, she was also able to take Casey for a few days at a time when he was on assignment. Dog-walking and dog-sitting services weren't cheap in Atlanta, but he would have hated to leave Casey in kennels.

He'd never actively looked for a dog. A pet had been the last thing on his mind. But Casey had kind of found him. One night when he'd been out running he'd noticed Casey lying by the side of the road. He'd hesitated for a few seconds—what did he know about dogs?—but as soon as he'd looked into the big black eyes he'd been sucked in. A few hundred dollars' worth of vet bills later he had become the proud owner of a terrier of unknown origin.

And it was an interesting partnership. Casey was more temperamental than most women he'd known. Snarky some days, loving on others, and absolutely determined to get his own way. On more than one occasion he'd grabbed hold of Donovan's trouser leg and dragged him towards the door when he wanted to be walked.

Hannah rang the doorbell and walked in. Her immediate attention went to the dog and she dropped to her knees and started tickling Casey behind the ears. 'Hey, boy. You're going to come with me for a while.' She picked up the plastic bag sitting on the counter, filled with Casey's favourite dog food. Donovan only merited a mere wave. 'Give me a call when you're due back, Donovan. Casey and I will be fine,' she clipped his lead onto his red collar and walked him out the door.

Donovan took a quick glance around the apartment, set his alarm and headed for the airport. It was a late flight and check-in wasn't until eleven p.m. but a few members of his team were already there when he arrived, checking in their specialised equipment. He could travel light, but the equipment required by the team was a logistical nightmare.

He was going through one of the check lists

when the voices around him stopped. He looked up. Dave and John were totally ignoring him, their attention focused elsewhere. Dave lifted his hand and waved. 'Over here, Grace,' his shout came out as something resembling a squeak, and the two other men smiled in amusement.

Donovan glanced across the concourse. And blinked. Twice. He could hear movie theme music playing in his head. What the hell?

It seemed like Grace was moving in slow motion—one shapely leg striding in front of the other—with every eye in the building on her. Her hair had been cut shorter by a few inches and a red wrap dress enhanced every curve. Her black jacket was clutched in one hand, and her suitcase dragged behind her.

Dave murmured, 'If that's what she looks like with her clothes *on*...'

Both sets of male eyes turned to face Donovan, their question apparent.

'Stop it, guys,' he said brusquely. 'Let's keep it professional.'

He kept repeating those words in his head because not one of his thoughts about Grace right now could be described as professional.

Why had she cut inches from her hair? He'd liked watching the way it had streamed down her back, finishing at the base of her spine, in the shower. But it bounced as she walked across the concourse in her stiletto heels. It was just touching her shoulders now, the colour more vibrant and a few little curls appearing. Darn it—it was sexier than before.

As she neared, his gaze was drawn to her green eyes. Now her face wasn't clouded by the expanse of hair, they stood out even more. Fixing on him with that deep colour.

Grace Barclay had attracted his attention before. But the Grace Barclay standing in front of him now was stunning.

Her case trundled to a stop and her face fell as she glanced at her companions. 'Are you ready to go?'

Donovan could sense her discomfort. It was just after eleven at night and she was dressed as if she were going to a power meeting in the office. He and the rest of the guys were dressed in jeans and baseball hats. He could curse. He should have given her a heads up about what dress code was expected on field assignments. He only hoped her heavy-duty case—that looked as if it held three weeks' worth of clothes—wasn't filled with suits and stiletto heels. They wouldn't be any use where they were going.

He was normally so good at this sort of thing. When he'd recruited anyone to his team in the past he'd always had a meeting with them, giving them a printed list of essential equipment for field assignments and some basic instructions about wherever they were travelling.

What was wrong with him? Why hadn't he done the same for Grace?

The little voice in his head wasted no time in telling him. *None of the other recruits were naked in the shower with you.*

He took a deep breath and swung his rucksack over his shoulder. 'We like to travel light, Grace, so there's no waiting around at the other side.' He gestured towards her case. 'Sorry, I should have given you a heads up. We'll spend most of our time in scrubs and they've been sent on with the rest of the equipment.'

She looked down at the huge case. 'Oh, I didn't realise.' She glanced at the rest of team's rucksacks. 'It's okay, guys. When we land you go on ahead. I'll wait for my case and meet you there.'

Dave shook his head. 'Oh, no, we don't mind waiting for you, Grace.' His voice was almost a drawl. Donovan shot him a look as the check-in girl gave him a nod.

'Hand over your passports. We'll get our seats allocated and head to the departure gate.' He signed a few forms about their other equipment, as Grace rustled through her leather bag for her passport.

Her scent was drifting up around his nostrils. Something new. Not like the perfume she'd been wearing as they'd hit the shower. This smelt like vanilla. The kind of cupcakes his mother had baked when he was a boy. She smelt good enough to eat.

She finally found her passport and pulled it from her bag. 'Sorry, Donovan.' She looked down at her clothes. 'I just assumed that because we were on business for the DPA it would still be office wear.' She tilted her head to the side, giving him a view of her smooth skin and a rueful smile. 'No matter what time of the day or night. But, hey, I guess we learn something new every day.'

She heaved her case up onto the check-in conveyer belt. There was no way this could be mistaken for carryon luggage.

He handed over the passports to the beautiful blonde desk clerk, who didn't look too impressed that she was being ignored. 'I guess we do,' he replied.

She had no idea how true those words were. He was trying to work out why he hadn't got a handle on Grace Barclay seven months ago. He'd noticed her, and had meant to find out more. But Donovan was a work first kind of guy. He didn't like things to interfere.

Still, seeing the reactions of Dave and John had sent the hackles up at the back of his neck. He'd wanted to rip their eyes from their sockets—not exactly rational behaviour, particularly around a woman he barely knew.

Grace Barclay was an adult and a professional. She was perfectly capable of looking after herself. She didn't need him to protect her, so why was that the way he felt around her?

He was trying not to stare at her curves. He'd already seen her naked—what more was there? But Grace wasn't just wearing this red dress, she *va-va-voomed* it. It covered every inch that it should. But its coverage was just great. It clung to the full curve of her breasts, the swing of her hips and the smooth swell of her backside. As for the tanned legs and black stiletto heels…

'Donovan, is something wrong? Did I forget something?'

She was staring at him, twiddling one strand of her shorter hair between her finger and thumb. Another 'tell' when she was nervous. It was cute. It was sexy.

He shook his head, trying to get his mind back on the job. 'Nice hairdo.' The words were out before he thought about them and her cheeks flushed in an instant.

'Thanks.' Her fingers were working overtime on that strand of hair. Any more and she would pull it clean from her head. 'My friends thought it would be more practical for a first field assignment.'

He raised his eyebrows and couldn't help but smile. 'Did they think the dress would be more practical too?'

He knew it. He knew there had been a makeover team involved. Grace looked fabulous, but he kind of preferred her the way she'd appeared twenty-four hours ago. When he'd been the only one who had noticed her.

Her shoulders sagged. 'Like I said, I wanted to look professional.'

The blonde behind the desk cleared her throat and handed over the boarding cards, her eyes drifting up and down the length of Grace's body with disapproval. Her gaze was so blatant he cringed.

But Grace didn't. She laughed. Out loud. And reached over and took the boarding cards from her hand. 'Thanks honey,' she quipped. 'I'll take care of these guys now.'

With a confidence Donovan hadn't seen before she swung her bag over her shoulder and started to walk towards Security. 'Come on, guys, let's go.' All eyes followed the swing of her hips and the rest of the team grabbed their bags and hurried after her.

By the time they reached Security Grace had emptied the contents of her bag, removed her gold necklace and put her shoes in the tray. She beeped as she walked through the scanner and stood patiently while the female security team scanned her with the wand. The scanner paused around her shoulder blade and she said a few quiet words to the staff member.

The woman reached up and pulled the stretchy red material out where indicated by Grace. It wasn't enough. A few seconds later she was asked to stand in the full-body scanner. What on earth was going on?

It took less than thirty seconds. The female guard viewed the scan and had a quick discussion with her counterpart. He nodded and she indicated to Grace to come out and handed her her shoes, talking away as if they were old friends. Grace was shrugging her shoulders and smiling. Donovan was concentrating so hard on what was happening between them he felt a sharp nudge at his back. 'Hurry up, buddy. The guard has signalled you through twice now.'

Donovan had already removed his belt, shoes, money and watch. There was no reason for him to beep. He hurried through and caught the last few words of the conversation. 'No problem, it happens every time...'

It had to be her scar. Questions were firing in his brain. There were lots of reasons people could beep at the airport. Metal plates in their bodies, other kinds of implants or devices. But the only scar he'd seen on her entire smooth skin had been the angry–looking one on her shoulder.

It just made him all the more curious. Grace didn't seem like the kind of girl to have had a knife wound. Maybe he was wrong? Maybe it was from a car wreck? A sports accident? A skiing mishap?

But it didn't matter how many 'what ifs' he planted in his brain. Donovan knew a knife wound when he saw one. He just wasn't sure he wanted to ask the question.

She was sliding her painted red toes into her

black stiletto. 'What next? Can we all go for a coffee somewhere and make some plans?'

Her voice jolted him. It was embarrassing. She wasn't having any problems focusing on the job. It was only him. Why hadn't he noticed the painted toes earlier?

'Sure. Let's go to the coffee shop. I'll recheck my emails and see if we've got any new information.'

She moved away and started chatting with John. He noticed the glances from passers-by as they walked through the terminal. Grace seemed to chat easily with people. She had a nice friendly nature, a killer smile and she appeared to be a good listener, all things that would make her an asset to the team. It would make her good with patients and give her the ability to integrate well with staff they might meet wherever they travelled.

They joined the queue and Grace frowned at the coffee selection.

'What's wrong? No skinny, caramel lattes?'

She wrinkled her nose. 'Oh, yeah, they've

got them. They just don't have any sugar-free caramel.'

'Is it important?'

'My hips seem to think so. And my thighs.'

'Not from where I'm standing.'

She met his gaze. It was only the briefest of seconds. Everything else around her seemed to fade into the background. All she could see was the cheeky twinkle in his eyes.

It panicked her. What did that mean? Was he joking with her or was he flirting with her?

Her friends may have given her a physical makeover but they hadn't done anything to sort out her woolly brain. Academically she could rival most of her colleagues but as for being street smart or worldly wise, she was neither. Never had been—never would be.

Her shoulder was a permanent reminder of that. The tiny tip of the knife still embedded in her tissues caused havoc every time she was near an airport scanner. The ER doc had done the best he could. It had been bad night in the ER and a surgeon hadn't been available. The tip was apparently right next to some nerves and unskilled removal could have resulted in damage. The scar was already going to be ugly, so she'd decided just to take the patch-up job, the antibiotics and go.

She tore her gaze away from Donovan's as she felt heat spread into her cheeks. She'd already used up her day's supply of sassiness on the desk clerk. As they moved along the line and grabbed coffee her eyes fixed on his well-worn jeans and slouchy T-shirt. Her fingers itched to touch it. It looked so soft, so comfortable—the kind of material that her pyjamas were normally made from.

She shifted on her heels. She'd felt a million dollars walking out the door tonight. It hadn't even occurred to her that the team would travel casual. Her heart had sunk like a stone when she'd realised how inappropriately dressed she looked in comparison to everyone else. This was going to be a long flight.

They settled at a table in the airport lounge, Donovan pulling out his laptop.

'This is what we know.' He gave Grace a little nod. 'Jessie Tanner, sixty-seven, reported to her physician five days ago. She had a whole range of symptoms that she claimed to have had for around three days. She was physically and mentally unwell. Dehydration, confusion, diarrhoea, and her skin was described as red and covered in bumps. Their initial diagnosis ranged from scarlet fever to measles then rubella. Her condition deteriorated very rapidly and she didn't respond to treatment.'

'Did we miss something with Ms Tanner? I don't ever remember her reporting symptoms like those.'

Donovan shook his head. 'She didn't. Not in any of the phone calls to the DPA. We checked our records—she's phoned us over four hundred times, for a whole variety of reasons.'

David and John let out simultaneous groans. John ran his fingers through his hair. 'Why do we get all the crazies?'

Donovan didn't acknowledge the comment, keeping focused on the facts. 'Our last call from Jessie Tanner was actually seven days ago. She never reported any symptoms then, just asked a range of questions about the bats that were near her home.' He lifted his eyes from the screen.

'That seems to have been the norm for Ms Tanner. Unfortunately, it looks like she might not have been as crazy as it seems.'

Grace leaned forward. 'What about the other patient—the child?'

Donovan paused, 'Actually, as of one hour ago, it's two patients. Since the provisional diagnosis by Frank, we sent an alert out to all medical centres. It seems that a maculopapular rash is appearing all over Northwest District in Florida. We still have the first child, an eight-year-old boy, but we also have a thirty-five-year-old woman.'

John took a deep breath. 'An epidemic? Are we prepared for that?'

'We'd better be.'

There was silence at the table as they all contemplated the words. It didn't matter how much experience he had, it didn't matter how many times he'd circled the globe to investigate some weird and deadly disease—in the DPA you were only as good as your last case. The truth here was he was investigating a disease he hadn't encountered before, none of the team had. There was no magic cure or vaccination against Marburg virus.

The sad fact was that surviving the virus could almost be down to luck. And Donovan hated it when things were left to unscientific rationales. He didn't work like that.

Their flight number was called and Donovan stood up, grabbing his bag. The casual atmosphere in his team was gone. They were all too concerned about what they might face when they arrived.

Grace's face was serious. He had to keep reminding himself this was her first fieldwork assignment. He had to stop thinking about what she'd looked like in the shower when the water had streamed down her soft skin and they'd been surrounded by steam…

No. Stop it. Be professional. Lots of new doctors thought they would love the fieldwork aspect of the DPA then quickly found out they hated every second. Things could be tough. Equipment wasn't always available, local staff might not be sufficiently trained and communications back to the DPA could be sketchy.

He'd have to remember that. Once Donovan arrived on the job he tended to shut out everyone around him. His drive, single vision and extreme focus were the aspects of his character he relied on. Trouble was, he forgot about supporting those around him. He expected everyone just to do their jobs. He didn't hand-hold. He didn't have time for that. So Grace had better not expect it. He needed her to hit the ground running and concentrate on the task.

The flight took off smoothly. Grace sat next to John and spent the forty-five-minute flight time talking about the virus and reading up notes on her tablet. It was just as well she wasn't next to him. He was conscious of every time she crossed and uncrossed her shapely tanned legs. At one point a black stiletto dangled from her painted toes. He had to drag his gaze away and concentrate on the strong black coffee served by the stewardess.

It was just before midnight by the time they arrived. The night was dark, hot and humid. The guys were ready to go straight off but found themselves hanging around the luggage conveyor belt, waiting for Grace's oversized case to arrive. It would be unkind to go on without her, Donovan kept telling himself as he paced around the airport.

The finally exited the arrivals hall and he looked around for their transport. 'Anyone see a card with DPA on it?'

John and David shook their heads. 'What about that guy on the phone over there? Doesn't his card say DPA?'

Grace pointed to a guy who was talking frantically on the phone, the crumpled sign in his hand. He must have thought he had missed them.

Donovan hurried over and tapped him on the shoulder. 'I think you're waiting for us.'

The guy cut his call. 'Donovan Reid, from the DPA?'

He nodded. 'Can you give us an update and take us straight to the hospital? Is it still two patients?'

The guy shook his head. He was unusually pale for a Florida local. Or maybe he was just feeling the lateness of the hour, like the rest of them. He gave a wave to couple of police officers near the doors.

'Two? You're joking? We're going to need a police escort. Latest count is thirty-five.'

He started walking towards the doors, not waiting for them to follow.

Donovan's strides lengthened. 'What do you mean, thirty-five? Where did they come from?'

The guy sighed as he pulled open the door of the police car. 'It seems that a kindergarten trip was at the state park caves five days ago.' His gaze swept around the team. 'I hope one of you guys is a paediatrician.'

Donovan felt his heart sink like a stone. Grace's face was a picture. It looked like her first assignment was going to be a baptism of fire.

CHAPTER FOUR

THE HOSPITAL WAS pure and utter chaos. People wandered everywhere, staff looked bewildered and hospital security seemed to have no idea what they were supposed to be doing.

Last time Grace had seen anything like this had been a nightmare shift in the ER as a resident during a major incident when there had been a pile-up on the nearby highway.

Three ambulances were in the bay outside, currently unloading patients. Hysterical parents were talking on mobile phones and one kid seemed in danger of wandering outside.

Grace grabbed the little hand in hers, thought about it for two seconds then lifted the toddler into her arms. The child looked around two and a half and wasn't in the least bit worried about being in the arms of a perfect stranger.

Donovan had moved into full team-leader

mode. The chaos didn't seem to worry him at all—in fact, he might even be thriving on it.

'John, I want you to find who is in charge of finding our primary source and co-ordinate with them. We need environmental controls in place to stop the spread of disease.' John nodded as if this were an everyday request and disappeared into the melee of people. 'David, set up communications with our labs and find out who is charge of the lab facilities here. I need you to start doing some provisional testing to move things along.' He spun round and caught sight of Grace, who had perched the toddler on the reception desk. 'Grace, what are you doing?'

'It seems like I'm looking after a lost child.'

He wrinkled his nose and shook his head. 'Hold on.' He walked over to the desk and grabbed the Tannoy system. 'Anyone lost a little boy, around two years old? Brown hair, red T-shirt.' His voice boomed around the waiting room and crowded ER. Heads turned from every direction. Donovan's wasn't a voice to ignore.

There was a shriek from the corner, where a woman was waiting with another child in her arms. 'Mason!' she yelled, as she pushed her way through the crowd with one arm outstretched and the other clamped around the other child. 'I'm sorry, I didn't even notice he'd vanished.' She promptly burst into tears as Grace handed the little boy over.

'Don't worry, he's fine and it's bedlam in here.' She squinted at the other child, who was older but whimpering and lethargic in his mother's arms, with a distinct tinge of yellow to his skin.

She glanced at Donovan but didn't wait for his response and bent down, 'Are you waiting for someone to see your son?

The woman nodded. 'We've been waiting for three hours.'

Grace did the sums in her head. It was after midnight. This woman had been here since nine p.m. with a sick kid. Not good.

She smiled. 'Okay, I'm going to show you to a cubicle then have a look at your son. Does he attend kindergarten? Was he on the trip the other day?'

Donovan seemed to be talking to three people at once, but he gave her a little nod and pointed her in the direction of an empty cubicle. Grace didn't need to take instruction from him; she knew exactly what she should be doing. The staff around here obviously couldn't cope with the influx of patients and would need the assistance of the DPA staff. She might not be a paediatrician but she was an experienced doctor and could do a basic assessment on a kid.

She dragged her suitcase behind her and dumped it in a corner. She could retrieve it later. Right now, she had a job to do.

The assessment took minutes. She charted the little boy's obs, took some bloods, set up an IV line and ordered some further tests.

By the time she joined Donovan a few minutes later he'd managed to acquire himself a clipboard, which he handed to her.

'Everything okay?'

She nodded. 'I'm pretty sure he's going to be another case. He's five and was on the cave trip with the kindergarten class and is clinically dehydrated and showing signs of jaundice.'

She looked around. 'Is there somewhere we can admit him?'

Donovan held up his hands. 'Right now, that's the million-dollar question. I've just spoken to the hospital director. He looks as if he's ready to have a heart attack. They are reorganising some patient areas to try and give us two ward areas for patients who are affected.'

'Do you have a number?'

The lines in his forehead seemed to have deepened in the last few minutes. 'Yeah, around thirty-seven. Thirty-eight if we count your latest. I've contacted the DPA for another team with some specialist paediatric staff. It'll be around twelve hours before they can get here, though.'

Grace understood. Until the rest of the team arrived, they were it. 'I'll manage,' she said swiftly. 'I can do a basic assessment and prescribe drugs and put in IVs for kids.'

Donovan was looking at her with those blue eyes. He should look tired because it was late. But he didn't. Instead, he looked invigorated. She'd heard that about him. About how he thrived on his job. Thrived on the pressure of it all.

She had to admit to feeling a little buzz herself on this first field assignment. But was the buzz from the job or from being around Donovan? The man was infectious. She liked the way that energy radiated from him. She liked the way his brain never seemed to stop thinking about the next task. Did he even have an off switch?

She looked at the list of names he'd given her. 'What do you want me to do with these?'

His voice was serious. 'I realise this is your first assignment, but I really need you to hit the ground running. You don't need to work up backgrounds or histories on any of the patients—John will be doing that. I need to check they've had all the bloodwork they should have, make sure the samples get sent to David at the lab, and keep an overall note on the condition of the patients. We need to keep on top of things here. The situation could become very volatile. Paediatric patients can deteriorate very quickly—we've already lost one older patient—and I'm assuming most people don't know that. If they did, we'd have a whole host of hysterical parents to deal with.'

His eyes swept around the room. 'This hospital only has sixty beds. It's usually only used for basic surgeries and medical complaints. Up until today there were only five paediatric beds. Anything major usually gets transferred to Panama City. If we have any kids that need ITU facilities, we'll need to transfer them.'

Grace nodded. She understood how serious the situation was, and how easily it could get out of control. For the next twelve hours Donovan needed a team he could rely on. It didn't matter that her stomach was currently churning. It didn't matter that she'd doubted for a few seconds if she could actually get the IV into the five-year-old's tiny vein. One look at that mother's face had given her all the determination she needed.

It was strange. Around twenty minutes ago all she'd wanted to do was drag her case somewhere, find her pyjamas and lie down for half an hour. She'd hit that point—the one that usually hit medics in the early hours, when it seemed as if everyone in the world was sleeping but them and they would kill for a bed. But the adrenaline surge had hit since then. Things were looking up. Maybe if she could grab some food she would get her second wind.

She took the clipboard and swallowed hard.

So many names, so much information to gather. She gave him her best smile. 'This will be fine, Donovan. I'll give you a shout if I run into any problems.'

He gave her a tight-lipped smile. Maybe not. Looked like she'd better deal with any problems herself. She pressed the clipboard to her chest. 'See you soon.' She kept the smile plastered on her face as she walked down the corridor. She could almost feel his eyes drilling a hole into her back.

She could do this. She could. Sleep was for amateurs.

He was watching her again. Watching the swing of her hips in that red dress. Darn it. He needed to tell her to change into a pair of scrubs. That way most of her curves would be hidden beneath the pale green material and he could concentrate on the things he needed to.

The Marburg Virus outbreak was much worse than first expected. One fatality already and a whole host of possibilities with a class of kinder-garten kids all exposed. He'd already reported to

Callum Ferguson, who was organising another team to come and assist. In the meantime, he had to try and get a handle on how to treat these patients and stop the spread of the virus. This place was a logistical nightmare. The lab facilities were basic. The staff were already run off their feet. Judging by the number of people in the ER they were going to run out of beds soon. The hospital facilities were fair, but there were no specialist facilities for any of the kids if their conditions deteriorated quickly.

Above all, he needed to communicate with the staff who were here. And he needed to do it quickly to make sure everyone was working from the same page.

John appeared at his side. 'We need to have a briefing for staff. Can you collect all the available staff on duty and we'll give them an overview of what we're dealing with and how they can contain the risk and stay safe?'

John moved quickly. He was used to this, and he was a professional. Donovan could rely on him.

In around ten minutes the staff were gathered

in one of the large nearby treatment rooms. There were around twenty of them—some nurses, some care assistants, two onsite doctors, admin staff and the hospital director. Most of them looked anxious and at least one woman was heavily pregnant.

Donovan stood in the doorway. 'Hi, folks. Thanks for stopping for a few moments. I'm Donovan Reid, a team leader at the Disease Prevention Agency. David Coles is working in your lab, John here will be doing case histories and Grace Barclay, one of our doctors, will be reviewing the patients and looking at symptom control.

'Most of you already know that we suspect we're dealing with the Marburg virus. We've had two confirmed laboratory cases and we're waiting for the results of others. Marburg virus can also be called Marburg haemorrhagic fever. We treat it the same way we treat other viral haemorrhagic fevers. Most patients are infected at source.' He glanced over at John. 'We're still establishing where that it is, but at the moment we suspect it's some bat caves in the local state park. Previous sources of infection for this virus have been African fruit bats.' All eyes in the room were watching him. He wanted to make this brief but comprehensible.

'The incubation period is between three and ten days, followed by a sudden onset of symptoms. These can include a rash over the trunk, nausea, vomiting, diarrhoea, chest pain and abdominal pain. More severe symptoms include jaundice, delirium, haemorrhaging, inflammation of the pancreas and liver failure.' He ran his hands through his hair. It didn't matter that there were over twenty people crammed into this room. Right now you could have heard a pin drop. Everyone was hanging on his every word.

'There is no magic cure for the virus. We don't have a vaccine against it. We can only treat the symptoms. Maintain fluid balances, give oxygen therapy, replace lost blood and clotting factors and treat any complications.' He looked around the staff. 'For everyone here, barrier nursing techniques have to be used in all cases. Any staff member exposed to body fluids is at risk. Protective gowns, gloves and masks have to be worn at all times. Take care with the disposal of needles, equipment and patient excretions.

'Patients who are worst affected should be placed in isolation if possible.' He held up his hands. 'I realise facilities here aren't ideal. But the people with the worst symptoms should be nursed in side rooms if possible. Parents have to be warned about the spread of disease. They have to be gowned, gloved and masked if they want to stay with their kids.'

The questions flew at him from all corners of the room.

'What if we've already been exposed?'

'How many people die from Marburg's?'

'Is this the only outbreak?'

'How long do the lab tests take?'

Donovan was calm, cool and collected. He answered everyone as best he could. The death rate could be terrifying. But he didn't want people running scared. There had already been a death here. Jessie Tanner hadn't been old. But the death of a sixty-seven-year-old was a lot less terrifying than the death of a kindergarten-aged kid. He had to try and keep things in perspective.

He kept everything brief and to the point. After around fifteen minutes most of the staff had returned to their stations.

Lucy Kirk, the head nurse, appeared at his side. 'I've got a couple of kids that need to be reviewed. Their symptoms are getting worse and they're not responding to their IV fluids. They can't stop vomiting and the fluids are coming out quicker than they're going in.' Her face was flushed and her hair had escaped from the elastic band at the nape of her neck.

Donovan looked up. 'Can't you ask Grace? She's supposed to be reviewing the patients.' He felt a little surge of annoyance. He'd just been asked to take part in a press conference for the local TV and radio stations. He'd done many of these in the past but knew he was supposed to run things by the communications department of the DPA first. Trouble was, he hadn't worked out what he was going to say yet—let alone put pen to paper.

Lucy shook her head. 'Grace is caught up with a kid with breathing difficulties. We've got six adults and thirty-four children as patients now.

Grace hasn't stopped for a second. We've already nicknamed her Superwoman. But she's only one person. Our regular doctor is spending most of his time trying to move the rest of our patients to other facilities.'

Donovan nodded quickly, running his hand through his hair. 'Okay, thank you. I'll be with you in two minutes.'

Lucy disappeared back to the ER while Donovan scribbled some quick notes for the press conference. He was being unreasonable. He couldn't really expect Grace, on her first assignment, to look after more than forty patients. Trouble was, things frequently worked out like that on DPA fieldwork trips.

He gowned, gloved and masked. It only took him a few minutes to review the kids and agree with Lucy's assessments. He wrote up some orders but, after looking around him, decided just to administer the anti-emetic IV shots to the kids himself. It didn't take long and he quickly disposed of his equipment and clothes.

He walked past an office where John was buried up to his neck in paperwork with two open laptops next to him. 'Okay? How are you getting on?'

John stood up. 'Exactly like we first suspected. The common denominator in everyone's story is the caves in the State Park. But they don't contain African fruit bats—they have Jamaican ones. What I can't work out is why Jamaican fruit bats have made it this far up state. They've been spotted in Key West before, but never this far northwest.'

'Have any of the state park staff reported being unwell?'

John pointed to the notes. 'I'm tracking down as many as I can. Two have already been admitted as patients. David's checking their blood results as we speak.' He gave a little smile, 'Grace seems to be taking samples quicker than he can analyse them.'

He mentally ticked the little box in his head. Another plus point for Grace. That reminded him. 'John, do you know where the supplies are? I'd like to get changed into a set of scrubs.' His voice drifted off. 'I need to tell Grace to get changed too.'

John shrugged. 'I think the boxes might be down at the lab.' He gave a little smile. 'I kinda like what Grace is wearing now.'

Donovan could feel his blood pressure start to rise. But John was watching him with a smirk on his face. He was playing him. Were his thoughts about Grace so apparent?

Darn it. He'd thought he was being cool. Romantic interludes between team members were never encouraged in the DPA. Team members were supposed to be focused and professional. Letting anything happen between him and Grace would be the quickest way to get her transferred off his team. And it would do nothing for her reputation.

Grace needed to establish herself as a solid fieldwork team member first. A year or two of experience in the field would cement her place in the agency and open a whole host of other opportunities for her.

And no matter how she looked in a red dress or how sexy her new haircut was, he had to keep his mind on the job.

The phone rang and John answered it. 'Yes,

yes, he's with me.' He glanced over at Donovan and started taking a few notes, which he passed over. Donovan read quickly. David had the lab tests running already. Out of twenty new samples—Grace really had worked quickly—the first few were already confirmed as Marburg virus. It would be another few hours before the rest were ready.

One of the admin staff appeared at his side. 'We've got problems.'

'What?'

'We're running out of IVs.'

'You're what?' He'd heard it all now. What kind of a hospital didn't have enough IV supplies?

'Most of the patients are really dehydrated. We're going through the infusion bags at a much quicker rate than normal and so far every single patient has an IV in place. We're going to have to send for some more equipment from one of the other local hospitals.'

'How quickly can it get here?'

She shrugged. 'Hopefully within a few hours.' She turned to leave, then spun back. 'Oh, and the other thing, the nurse supervisor said to let you know that she can't get enough extra nurses to cover all the shifts.'

Could this night get any worse? He took a deep breath. 'There will be some nursing staff coming down from Atlanta. Hopefully they'll be able to fill any gaps.'

She gave a nod. 'I'll let Lucy know, thanks.'

His stomach growled loudly and John smiled. Food. When was the last time they'd eaten? Probably in the airport before they'd left Atlanta.

'There must be a canteen around here. Can I get you something to eat, John?'

He nodded. 'Anything. And coffee. Black and lots of it.'

'No problem, see you in five.'

He walked along the corridor, his eyes looking through all the open doors in the hope of a glimpse of red. Finally, he heard the click-clack of her stiletto heels on the floor to his right. Her feet must be killing her by now.

He could hear her talking to one of the mothers, offering some reassurance about the condition of her child. 'Grace, can I borrow you for a second?'

She spun around and gave him a smile. At first glance she still looked as fresh as she had at the airport. But that had been hours ago now. And on closer inspection he could see the fatigue hiding behind the glaze in her eyes.

He put his arm through hers. 'Walk with me for a second.'

'Why, where are we going?'

Her legs kept pace with his as they turned the corner. 'Any place that serves food.'

She stopped walking and frowned. 'The hospital kitchen only serves the patients. Staff have to eat elsewhere.' She pressed a hand to her stomach. 'I already asked.'

'Is there someplace close by?'

'There's apparently a coffee stand across the street, some vending machines in the ER and a twenty-four-hour diner on the corner.'

'But nothing on site?' His brain was working overtime. They had a potential deadly virus with patients needing round-the-clock care and staff needing round-the-clock facilities.

She shook her head and he smiled. 'Well, things

are about to change around here. Do you know where the kitchen is?'

She nodded and pointed down the hall. 'What are you going to do, Donovan?' She followed as he marched towards the kitchen door. 'We just got here—don't go upsetting people.'

He shot her a smile—she was really cute when she was worried. 'Don't worry, Grace. I'm just going to get us some food.'

The kitchen door opened with a crash and a formidable woman scowled at him and started talking in rapid Spanish. He walked over, his arm extended firmly in front of him. Donovan Reid knew exactly how to use his charm to full effect.

'Hi, there. I'm Donovan Reid from the DPA. I understand you're in charge of the kitchen?'

The woman nodded, still scowling. 'I'm Mara.' She waved her other hand, 'And staff aren't allowed in here.'

He kept smiling and didn't let go of her handshake, instead wrapping his other hand over hers. 'It's a real pleasure to meet you. I'm sure you're aware we've got some really sick patients. And I'm expecting a whole host of other staff to arrive to help us take care of them.' He gave her his best smile. 'I absolutely don't want to give you any extra work.' He pointed over towards some empty workspace. 'So, if it's okay with you, I'll just get my staff to come in and fend for themselves.'

He could see her taking a deep breath, ready to tell him exactly where to go. So he spoke as quickly as he could.

'Obviously, at this time it's really important that my staff don't leave the premises while they are on duty. I don't want an emergency situation when all my staff are at the diner across the street. Can you imagine how dangerous that could be?'

He could see her eyes widen and her brain start to digest his words.

He dropped her hand and moved over to the workspace. 'You just tell me exactly where we won't interfere with your routine and I'll make sure my staff stay clear. I mean, some of us have been up all night travelling, and won't be getting any help for another…' he glanced at his watch '…six hours. It's important I keep my staff hydrated, don't you think?'

He could see Grace watching him out of the corner of his eye. Her arms were folded across her chest and she was leaning against the wall with her eyebrows partially raised. The bamboozling seemed to have worked. Mara looked lost for words.

Time to keep the momentum going. He started opening a few cupboards. 'Do you have coffee, Mara? I'd like to make some for my staff.'

He kept moving, looking through cupboards. Everything he'd just said was true. He didn't want his staff leaving the premises when they were on duty, and it didn't seem too much to ask to let the staff use the kitchen to prepare food. But Mara looked like the kind of woman not to be tangled with. He only hoped she didn't notice he was holding his breath.

Mara moved, her round body almost at odds with her lightning feet. She pulled open a door and thumped a tin of coffee down on the counter, pulling a glass coffee pot from another cupboard. 'I don't want anyone touching my range.' She eyed him for a few seconds before adding, 'I have bagels. And I can make some eggs.'

He walked over and slid an arm around her shoulders. 'Mara, that would be wonderful. Thank you so much.'

She moved sideways. 'Make your own coffee,' she muttered as she started cracking some eggs into a pan.

Donovan breathed a sigh of relief as he filled up the coffee pot with water. Grace appeared at his side with a grin on her face. 'Oh, very smooth,' she murmured quietly.

'I was, wasn't I?' With the coffee on and percolating he moved to the refrigerator and grabbed some milk.

His phone beeped and he pulled it from his pocket, half smiled and gave a little shake of his head.

She arched her eyebrows at him and he shrugged, 'It was Hannah.'

'How is Casey?'

'Apparently pining for me.'

She gave a little laugh. 'Well, somebody's got to.'

Grace picked up some mugs, plates and cutlery. Mara was slicing and toasting bagels now with ruthless efficiency. No wonder she didn't like people in her kitchen.

'There's a staffroom down the hall. I'll go and find David and John and meet you there.' She glanced over at Mara and gave him a wink as she disappeared out of the door.

Donovan smiled. He couldn't help it. Just when he least expected it, Grace did something like that. It was like at the airport, when the check-in girl had looked at her as if she had been something on the bottom of her shoe. Grace had just lifted her chin and acted as though she owned the world. He liked it. He liked it a lot.

There was a thump on the counter in front of him. Toasted bagels and a large bowl filled with scrambled eggs. His stomach growled loudly again. It smelled delicious—he hadn't realised just how hungry he was.

That seemed to be the way Mara worked. Thumping. He gave her the playboy smile again. 'Thank you so much, Mara, that was really good of you.' He grabbed the plates and the coffee pot and juggled them in his hands as he backed out the door.

Grace was handing over a five-dollar bill to John as he reached the staffroom. 'What's going on?'

Grace rolled her eyes and pulled up a chair. 'I lost a bet.'

'What bet?' He handed out the bagels and filled his with scrambled egg.

John grabbed the coffee pot and started pouring the tantalising liquid into mugs. 'I bet Grace as soon as we arrived that you would commandeer the kitchen, some way or another.'

She laughed, her head going back and revealing the paler skin of her neck. 'I'd already run into Mara when I was looking for a bottle of water. I thought you didn't have a hope of getting in there.'

David and John clinked their coffee cups conspiratorially. 'Let me tell you, Grace, you lucked out with this team. Donovan *always* manages to find us food. Rae Jenkins's team? Last time they were out in the field they ate granola bars for three days.'

Donovan laughed as he took a bite of his bagel. Delicious. Mara could thump around all day if she gave him access to food that tasted like this. 'It's true, you know. The other team complained about it for weeks.'

Grace was looking around the table, obviously trying to figure out if they were playing her or not.

David rolled his eyes. 'I can't do without food. I get all cranky these days if I don't eat. It's not pretty.' With his white shock of hair, David was the oldest member of the team. He was worth his weight in gold.

'How are things in the lab?'

'Don't worry about the lab. I'll be fine. Worry about staff on the floor—there aren't enough.'

Donovan frowned. 'I know. I spoke to the hospital director. They're just not set up for a major incident like this. Trouble is, to move all these patients elsewhere would probably take the National Guard. We have to manage as best we can.' He looked over at Grace. She'd finished eating and was sipping her coffee quietly. 'How about you, Grace?'

Her tongue ran along her lips. She was thinking before she spoke. Was that because she was unsure of herself or because he'd snapped at her earlier? She still hadn't managed to get changed into scrubs and the high humidity in Florida was making her hair start to frizz. But even he knew better than to point that out to a woman who'd had a makeover less than twenty-four hours ago.

She spoke quietly. 'I've got three kids I'm quite worried about. How long until the other team arrives?'

His brain was ticking rapidly as he tried to remember what was in her file. Grace didn't have much experience in paediatrics apart from a stint in the ER as an attending. She was obviously anxious for the team of more specialist staff to arrive. He should have thought of that.

'I'll come and review them with you before I go to the press conference.'

She let out her breath, her shoulders relaxing and rigid fingers loosening around the mug in her hands. She gave a grateful little nod of her head.

Their eyes met. It was a moment. A flicker. A connection.

Something about that shade of green, not pale and insipid, not deep enough to be emerald, but something in the middle. More like the colour of the ocean on a bright summer's day. It was holding him. It was dragging him in.

She blinked. Now he was looking at her long dark eyelashes and the way they framed her eyes perfectly. She was tired—he could see the faint lines around her eyes, the little furrows across her brow. She'd tried to capture her silky curls back in a ponytail. But its new shorter style didn't want to comply. A few random strands were still bouncing around her shoulders.

He dragged his gaze away. His brain should be computing what he was going to say at the press conference, not being distracted by the woman opposite.

John helped himself to a second toasted bagel. 'Are you ready for the onslaught?'

He focused. It was time to keep all his attention on the job. 'What onslaught?'

'The five hundred and fifty questions you're going to get about the bats. Maybe we should start calling you Dr Doolittle?'

Donovan shifted in his chair. 'Where are we

with the bats? Do we have confirmation of the primary site yet? When can we collect samples?'

John shook his head. 'The state parks are giving me the runaround right now. I think they've been inundated by calls from frantic parents. About the only thing I've managed to accomplish so far is to get them to put a temporary closure notice on the caves. What I haven't managed to do yet is secure us entry to collect samples.'

Donovan sat back in his chair. 'You are joking, right? I'm going to a press conference, and I've got to tell the world we have an outbreak of Marburg virus but we haven't even managed to collect samples yet?'

John lifted his hands. 'Doing the best I can, Donovan. These things take time—whether we like it or not. And Marburg virus is tricky. Most people have never heard of it. It's not like smallpox, with a six-hundred-page plan ready to download from our website *if* there was ever an outbreak anywhere. Our trouble is we didn't really plan for this.'

John was right. Donovan knew he was right. But it didn't make things any easier.

He pulled a piece of paper from his pocket. 'Okay, guys, keep me posted on any changes and I'll let you know how things go once I've been thrown to the lions. Here are the details of our accommodation. No doubt it will be a luxury five-star, all-inclusive resort.'

There was a collective groan around the table. The DPA didn't like to waste money on staff accommodation. They were lucky they hadn't been expected to pitch tents.

He lifted up his coffee mug, 'To teamwork.'

'To teamwork.' The mugs clinked together. 'Here's hoping the rest of the staff arrive soon.'

CHAPTER FIVE

GRACE CHECKED THE list again. The words were beginning to swim in front of her eyes. She still had two children to check over then another review of the three she was worried about.

She felt a warm hand at the base of her spine. Not low enough to be cheeky but something familiar. Donovan's head rested on her shoulder for a second. 'Are we still awake?' he groaned.

'Barely.' She turned round to face him, dislodging his chin from its resting place. If she wasn't getting to sleep, neither was he. She was still worried about these kids.

'Spoilsport.' He arched his back and it gave a loud crack.

'Yeurgh.' She raised her eyebrows. 'You should see a doctor about that.'

He wagged his finger at her. 'Don't even go there.' He rested his elbows on the nurses' station. 'I'm sorry I've been so long. The good news is I've found another four nurses, the equipment and supplies have been sorted and it's only two hours until the other team arrives. The bad news is I've got the press conference in twenty minutes.'

She let out a long slow breath. It was difficult to be patient when all she wanted to do was grab the nearest bed and lie down. But that was the thing—there *were* no empty beds now. All sixty beds were filled. All with patients with suspected Marburg virus.

There were a few cases she suspected were false alarms, but nonetheless all samples were currently lined up and waiting for David to test them in the lab.

She pushed her clipboard towards him. 'Well, my bad news is we're full. No beds. The last two were filled as soon as the previous patients were transferred to another local hospital.'

'The hospital director managed to get all the other patients transferred?'

She nodded. 'He's been great—even though he looks as if he's about to have a heart attack.' She lifted her hands and let out a sigh. 'We are now officially the Marburg hospital.'

He bent over the list. 'You've got through all these patients?' His voice rose and she felt a little tingle across her skin. Was that a note of admiration in his voice?

She tried not to smile. 'Yes, by the time I get to them John has done the patient history and background. I've been taking care of all the clinical components.'

'Show me the children you're worried about.'

She nodded and grabbed the sets of notes she'd put aside. The admiration for her hard work would only take her so far. She started down the corridor. 'I've done some moving around. The three patients I'm concerned about are all in single rooms down here. All children.' She lowered her voice. 'All on the kindergarten trip.'

She heard him suck in a breath. She knew exactly where his mind was going. They really needed access to those caves. They needed to identify where the virus had originated and get plans in place to help stop the spread.

She stopped at the entrance to one of the rooms.

Donovan was concentrating so hard that he wasn't paying attention and walked straight into the back of her.

Her body shot forward, her hands still clutching the clipboard, with no time to try and break her fall as her feet started to disconnect from the floor. The green rubber flooring loomed beneath her eyes.

A warm arm grabbed around her waist with such intensity that her breath was taken clean away from her. She was yanked back hard, straight into the chest of Donovan Reid.

'Grace, I'm sorry. I wasn't paying attention.'

She couldn't speak for a few seconds. All the air had shot out of her lungs. When she finally managed to suck in a breath and relax back against him, all she could do was laugh.

It was a nervous laugh. An I'm-feeling-something-I-shouldn't kind of laugh.

Like the heat of someone else's warm skin seeping straight through her thin scrubs. The feel of the rise and fall of his chest muscles against her shoulder blades. She should have kept her dress and her heels on. The thicker material and little more height wouldn't have left her quite so exposed. She could feel the outline of other parts of his body too.

His hand was still locked around her waist, holding her close to him. It didn't matter that he'd already seen every part of her. It didn't matter she'd been naked in a shower with him. This was up close and personal. This felt even more intimate than that.

This was the kind of position you assumed with a lover when you were looking out at a setting sun and glorious landscape. This was how you stood before he murmured in your ear and started to nuzzle around your neck. This wasn't a position for a public setting.

She jumped forward, pushing her hair out of her eyes. The shorter style was beginning to annoy her. It was at that in-between stage. Not quite long enough to stay in a ponytail band and not quite short enough to go without.

Donovan was looking at her with a strange expression on his face. His brow was furrowed but his blue eyes were fixed completely on her. Was he about to say something?

Then she got it. He felt it too.

It wasn't just her. She wasn't going crazy.

All those mad midnight dreams about Donovan Reid in a semi-naked state weren't as wasted as she'd thought. In her head he'd always been miles out of her league. The man hadn't even noticed her, let alone spoken to her. But things were definitely changing. He looked just as confused as she felt.

She broke the gaze, staring at the clipboard. Patients. Let's talk about patients.

'Okay Donovan, there's three kids I'm worried about—and you already reviewed them earlier. All aged five, all on the kindergarten trip. David has just confirmed that all three have Marburg virus. Jacob and Sophia are both showing signs of jaundice. Both are now having bloody diarrhoea. Breathing is becoming laboured and I'd really recommend that we transfer both these kids to the ICU in Panama City. Ryan is also deteriorating rapidly. Pulse is rising, blood pressure dropping and oxygenation rate is decreasing. Although all of these kids have had anti-emetics, they've had limited effect. All three kids are still vomiting and severely dehydrated.'

She took a deep breath. The words had just rattled out. She hadn't been able to stop them. She had real concerns about these three kids. Donovan was watching her carefully. The last thing she wanted was for him to think she couldn't cope. Because she could.

But every instinct in her body told her that these kids needed specialist treatment. She knew the death rate for Marburg could be as high as ninety per cent, but those rates were based on Marburg in countries that weren't as developed as the US. With all the facilities available, these kids had to have a better chance than that.

He reached out his hand and took the charts from her hands. 'Let's not waste time. Go, and try and arrange to get these kids airlifted out of here. You'll have a fight on your hands—first, with ICU at Panama City to accept three kids with an infectious disease and, second, with the air crew.' His hand rested on her back. 'It won't be the first fight you'll have like this, Grace, but I have confidence you'll make the case.'

His eyebrows were raised. It was almost like drawing a line in the sand. Setting her a challenge. Her stomach flipped over.

His eyes were serious, but the corners of his mouth were edging upwards. He was trying not to smile. And she was trying not to react to the feel of his hand on her back.

His fingers were inches from her scar and the heat emanating from his hand through her thin scrub top was making her skin tingle and the scar area itch.

The wound never bothered her, never caused her any problems—except, of course, at airports. While it had been healing the itch had driven her mad. Probably because that tiny part of her shoulder blade seemed like the most inaccessible part of her body. No matter how she twisted and turned, her hands just couldn't reach the spot. She'd ended up rubbing her shoulder blade up and down a wall instead.

The fingers moved, shifting their position on her back. 'Grace, are you okay?'

Heat rushed into her cheeks, Donovan had given her some clear instructions. She didn't have time to dither. She had to get on and do the job, prove herself as a responsible member of the team.

His fingers were still in contact with her body so she took a step forward to get out of reach.

'No problem, I'll get on the phone straight away.' She started to walk down the corridor. She'd no idea where she was going. There was a perfectly good desk, chair and phone at the nurses' station where they'd been standing but she needed some space. She needed some distance.

She could almost feel his eyes burning a hole into her back. As she rounded the corner she glanced back just in time to see him pull his eyes away and look down at the files in his hands.

She swallowed. She hadn't missed anything with these kids. She knew she hadn't. But she was worried. Their condition was deteriorating and they needed more support. So why was her stomach doing flip-flops?

She was nervous. She couldn't help it. She wanted Donovan to think she was a capable member of the team. It seemed so important that he respect her work abilities above anything else.

She had to prove to him she was a worthy member of his team. She wanted his respect. There had been a moment in the isolation room, when she'd told him what she remembered about Marburg virus, that he'd looked at her—*really* looked at her for a few seconds. It had almost been as if he was seeing her for the first time.

And there had been something. Whether it had been admiration, respect or just downright curiosity, she'd liked it.

She wanted it to happen again.

Even now, from the second she'd set foot in the airport, she had sensed something else. She wasn't as street smart as some. Her wound was proof positive of that.

But she didn't use the art of flirtation as a means to anything else. She wasn't skilled at those techniques and sometimes she wondered if she even read things the way she should.

In any other world, if she were any other person, she could swear that Donovan Reid had been flirting with her sometimes. Had been looking at her in a way that hadn't been entirely professional. And she liked it. She liked it a lot.

Up until yesterday she hadn't featured on this guy's radar at all. She may have admired him from afar. He may have said a few things that had hinted he had noticed her. But that had probably been just to soothe her ego, keep her sweet while she was on his team.

She wasn't a blonde supermodel. Not like the last girl he'd dated. Or anything like any of the others he'd been rumoured to wine and dine. She was just Grace Barclay, doctor at the DPA.

But when he'd held her gaze a few times and looked at her, it had felt like so much more. It had made her skin tingle and the blood race through her veins. He'd looked at her in the shower when they'd both been naked. He'd looked at her at the airport when she'd had her mini-makeover. The first time she'd barely been able to meet his gaze. The second time she'd felt more confident, more ready to deal with it.

Donovan Reid interested in her? She couldn't wipe the smile from her face or the tingles that were sweeping over her skin.

She picked up the phone. Now it was time to be charm personified. Now it was time to develop some of her persuasive skills to get these kids somewhere appropriate.

And maybe she could use those persuasive skills later…

The room was stifling and it was packed. It was Florida in the middle of summer and the air-conditioning wasn't working. Sweat was starting to run down his back, he only hoped his shirt wasn't sticking to his back.

Worse still, there were no windows. No outside view to escape from. Two doors, both surrounded by people and both closed. It made his skin prickle. Maybe he wasn't sweating because of the temperature, maybe he was sweating because he couldn't see the outside. His mind was retreating into the six-year-old-boy space again and he pressed his lips tightly together, willing it back to the present.

He wasn't a six-year-old boy. He was an adult. And all his rational sensibilities were telling him he was fine. The room wasn't entirely comfortable but there was a clear exit, *two* clear exits. Well, not entirely clear. But visible.

That should be enough. That should be enough to allow him to continue through this. The last thing he wanted to do in the middle of a packed room full of reporters was have a panic attack.

He'd always managed to stave them off. He'd always managed to talk himself out of them, even when all the symptoms and sensations had been there, he'd recognised them and tried to rationalise things in his brain.

A team leader with panic attacks in enclosed spaces would be no use in the DPA. You never knew what situation or set of environmental circumstances you could end up in. Doctors in the DPA had to be able to deal with everything. Team leaders? They had to deal with the impossible.

He couldn't let his childhood traumas interfere with his present-day life. He had no time for this. It didn't make sense. Not even to him. Sure, six hours trapped in an elevator was terrifying for a child. But it didn't really feature as traumatic. In his experience he'd met lots of people who'd had a million experiences more terrifying than his. It almost had him feeling embarrassed that his body reacted this way—in a way he couldn't control.

He took a few long deep breaths, letting the air hiss out slowly through his lips. He'd read his DPA-agreed statement around thirty minutes ago. It had been hastily written on an unused chart then faxed to the department. He'd thought he could be in and out of here in ten minutes. But he should have known better. The reporters had other ideas. They were out for blood. And by the look of it—his.

The questions were coming thick and fast. 'Have you identified the source?'

'Marburg virus has been known in the past to come from the African fruit bat. While we've identified bats before in Key West, that type of bat has never been found here. We have, however, identified Jamaican fruit bats in the area. Further investigations are taking place.'

'But weren't all the kids that were affected on a kindergarten trip to the national park? Should the park be closed?'

He shifted in his seat. This was where things

got difficult. 'Our investigators are taking detailed histories from all people who have contracted the virus. We are looking at any and all commonalities. Until the investigation is complete I can't make any further comment.'

What I really mean is the park authorities still haven't let us in there. It was beyond frustrating. All establishments had their own protocols but nothing was supposed to get in the way of a DPA investigation. Federal law stated they had jurisdiction. It just didn't seem apparent right now. For some agencies the wheels of time seemed to move slower than shifting sands.

'What can you tell us about the first victim? The woman who died? We heard she called the DPA on a regular basis.'

How on earth did they know that? He did his best to smile sweetly, while racking his brains. Someone from the DPA must have leaked the information. There would have to be an investigation.

'The first confirmed case of Marburg virus was Jessie Tanner, age sixty-seven, from Northwest District in Florida. She has phoned the DPA in the past, but I can confirm she never reported any clinical signs that were related to Marburg virus.'

This was a nightmare. The sooner he could get out of here and on the phone to the Director of the DPA the better.

'Is it true that there was another kindergarten trip at the same site the day after this one?'

His skin started to prickle as a chill swept across his body. That was the absolute last thing he wanted to hear. He kept his face as bland as possible. 'We've not yet been notified of that possibility.'

He wanted out of there. He wanted out of there as soon as possible to check those facts. He wanted to make sure another thirty kids weren't at risk.

The door at the side of the room burst open. 'Donovan! I need you, now!'

In any other set of circumstances he might have been grateful for the interruption, relieved even. But Grace's face was as white as a sheet. The head of every reporter in the room turned to her and in one action the whole crowd seemed to surge towards her.

Donovan couldn't take his eyes off her. Her previously coiffed hair was sticking out in all directions, her scrubs were rumpled, but the thing he noticed most was her unwavering focus.

He stood up and pushed his way through the crowd. 'Out of my way!'

It was only seconds until he reached her, but it felt like for ever. The reporters were too busy chasing the story, rather than thinking of the emergency situation. Grace's hands and legs were spread at the doorway, firmly stopping any of the reporters getting through. Her chin was set determinedly, but her eyes were scanning the crowd frantically, looking for Donovan.

He placed his hand over hers in the doorway and she grabbed it quickly and pulled him through with a force he underestimated, kicking the door closed behind her.

He felt the first flush of fresh air surround his skin.

'Now,' she said, her feet running a few steps down the corridor, giving him no time to think. As soon as the door had closed behind him he was instantly aware of the cardiac-arrest alarm sounding in this part of the hospital. It had been years since Donovan had heard one. It had been years since Donovan had responded to one in this kind of environment, but all his automatic medical senses kicked into place.

He was right behind her as she ran into a room, dragging an emergency trolley from the corridor behind her. There was one nurse, with a knee on the bed, counting out loud as she did chest compressions on the small boy.

Donovan did a double take. 'Where is everyone?' In all his years he'd never seen this. Whenever a cardiac arrest alarm sounded in a hospital setting, everyone responded. It was an unwritten rule. Only one nurse and Grace? It was unheard of.

The little body had two IVs running, one with fluids, one with bloods, and from the signs on the bed he'd already been haemorrhaging.

Donovan moved to the top of the bed, taking the most obvious position of airway support. He released the brake on the bed, pushing it forward and lifted the headrest out of place. He grabbed the Ambu bag from the top of the trolley, connected the oxygen and inserted a child-sized airway to maintain the little boy's respiratory status. This was a temporary measure. The child should be intubated but he couldn't see the equipment he needed right now.

Grace was connecting the monitoring equipment and defibrillator around the nurse's hands. 'Sorry, Donovan, I needed urgent assistance.'

'Where on earth is the rest of the staff?'

'There are four of them outside, transferring one of the kids onto a helicopter.'

'You arranged the transfers?' He was surprised she'd managed to pull it off. Grace was rising in his estimation all the time.

'Yeah, with a few conditions.' She waved her hand. 'We'll get to them later?'

As for getting him out the press conference? It wasn't ideal. The press would be all over this like a rash. But patients always came first. And Grace had looked as if she couldn't care less about the members of the press. She'd just known she'd needed help.

He couldn't even begin to let himself acknowledge how panicked he'd begun to feel in that room. Right now it felt safer to recognise that Grace had interrupted the conference to get help. Safer for him at least.

She finished connecting the electrodes to the little boy's body. 'There's a sick adult on the other side of the ward. Two staff are inserting a chest tube.' She gave her head a little shake. 'We just don't have enough staff for the poor condition of these patients, Donovan.' She opened up the IV nearest her, quickly moving back to the patient. 'This blood isn't going in quickly enough.'

Donovan nodded in agreement. Tyler Bates. Five years old. He'd reviewed him with Grace a few hours ago and recommended he be transferred as soon as possible to ICU. The little boy was deathly pale. It was clear he'd started to haemorrhage. Rapid fluid replacement, both blood and clotting factors, would be needed to help him survive.

'Hands off.' The nurse stopped what she was doing and immediately started running the cryoprecipitate to aid blood clotting through another IV.

Donovan turned his eyes to the monitor. His

hand was routinely squeezing the Ambu bag to push air into his lungs. He identified the heart rhythm immediately. 'VF. Shock him, Grace.'

She didn't hesitate and set the level on the machine. 'Stand clear.' He'd no idea how long it had been since Grace had resuscitated someone—let alone if she'd ever resuscitated a child before—but she made it look as if she did this every day. Now she had the additional support she'd needed for his airway, she was the coolest person in the room. He lifted his hands away from the little boy's face.

The little boy's body shuddered and they watched the flickering blue line for a few seconds. The unruly squiggle, ventricular fibrillation, had shown them his heart wasn't beating properly—just quivering in his chest. There was few seconds of hesitation then the squiggle changed. One little blip, slowly followed by another.

'Give him some adrenaline.' The child's heart rate was still too low but at least he had one. In another minute Donovan would have needed to intubate, but now the little boy gave an involuntary cough and his temporary airway was expelled. Donovan turned the oxygen supply up full and pulled a mask over his face, keeping the Ambu bag close by in case he needed it again.

The slow heartbeat took a few minutes to gradually pick up its rate. Their biggest concern now would be helping this little boy maintain his pulse and blood pressure while they tried to replace his lost blood products.

Two other nurses appeared at the door. 'What happened?' one of them asked.

Grace gestured to the bed. 'Tyler arrested.' She looked up. 'Did Jacob get transferred?'

They nodded. One of the nurses moved over towards the bed and started clearing away the used supplies, while the other checked Tyler's blood pressure. 'The medevac team did mention something about other doctor and nurses.' She raised her eyebrows in question at Grace.

Donovan caught the glance between them. Tyler's breathing was becoming steadier. 'Grace?'

A little colour flushed her cheeks as she checked the rate on the IV delivering blood to

Tyler. 'I might have agreed to a few conditions for the transfer,' she mumbled.

Donovan felt his ears prick up and cool wave wash over his skin. 'And what might they be?'

He couldn't even begin to imagine how Grace had managed to arrange the transfers so quickly. He had visions of the DPA budget being blown out of the window, with his name attached to it.

He straightened up, because she hadn't answered. 'Grace, what did you agree to?'

She was checking Tyler's heart rate again. Her eyes glanced quickly over at him then skittered away. 'I might have agreed to put a team into the hospital at Panama City.'

He sucked in a breath. They already had another team headed here. Three teams? Working on the same outbreak? Well, that would make DPA history.

'You phoned the request in?'

She licked her lips. 'Yes.' She still wasn't looking at him.

'And they agreed?' He could see how nervous she was, how edgy.

And he wasn't mad at her. He wasn't. Patient

care came first. And if this was the only way to get the kids transferred to the facilities they needed, then so be it.

He could make the argument in the director's office later.

She took a deep breath and finally looked him in the eye. Her words tumbled out. 'I'm sorry, Donovan. I said you insisted. I said you authorised it. I didn't know what else to do. They didn't have the expertise at Panama city ICU and said the only way they could accept the kids was if they had specialist help. They made the case that they had other patients to protect. I couldn't think of a way around it. So I just said yes. And I gave your name.'

She'd moved, and was standing in front of him now. She was breathing quickly; he could see the little pulse throbbing at the base of her neck. She looked as if she might cry. The nurses looked up, both with amused expressions on their faces. Tyler heart rate was steady now. 'I'm going to talk with Tyler's mom,' said one. 'I'm going to get some sheets to change the bed,' said the other, and they both exited the room at top speed.

Another doctor appeared at the door. He was one of the regular hospital staff. He looked at the equipment. 'Sorry, I couldn't respond to the arrest call. The chest drain is in now and my patient is stabilised. Can I take over in here? The second medevac phoned to say they'll be here in ten minutes. Can you write up Tyler's notes about what just happened?'

Grace hadn't moved. She was still standing in front of Donovan. Looking at him with those big green, trembling eyes. 'Of course,' he said quickly, picking up Tyler's case notes and grabbing her hand to pull her from the room.

The corridor was quiet. There was only him and her. But it seemed too open, too exposed. He pulled her towards the nearest on-call room and closed the door behind them.

Now it was definitely just him and her. He hadn't even flicked the light on in the room. He could almost sense that she wouldn't want him to.

He put his hands on her shoulders. 'Grace, are you okay?'

It wasn't just her eyes that were trembling, it

was her whole body. Did she really think he'd be annoyed about her decision?

Then it hit him. And he didn't hesitate. He wrapped his arms around her and pulled her close against his chest.

'You've never resuscitated a child before, have you?'

The stifled sobs told him all he needed to know. His free hand stroked the top of her head. A waft of fruit came in his direction, she obviously used citrus-scented shampoo. 'You did good, Grace. Real good. Tyler's back.'

She shook her head against him. Her words were muffled, 'But I panicked, Donovan. I panicked. No one responded to the call and I knew I couldn't do everything with just one nurse. I didn't mean to interrupt the conference. I know I should have checked about the other team. But I didn't want you to think I was incapable.' Her voice was even quieter, 'I panicked.'

He walked her backwards towards the single bed against the wall, letting her sit down on it. He kneeled in front of her, taking his hands and putting them on her cheeks, tilting her head up.

He knew all about panic.

Her eyelashes were damp, her cheeks flushed. He could feel the slight perspiration at the base of her neck. 'Grace, I don't care about the promise of the other team. I don't care about the interrupted press conference. All I care about is that Tyler Bates's heart is beating again and he's about to get transferred to an ICU.'

She was trying to draw a breath, but her whole body was shuddering. 'I should have been able to handle an arrest on my own. I'm a doctor. I shouldn't need any assistance. I should have managed.' Her eyes were fixed on the floor.

He shook his head. 'Grace, look at me. *Look* at me.'

Her eyes finally lifted again. 'I don't know how I would have managed a paediatric arrest on my own.'

Her lips tightened. 'You're just saying that. You're just saying that to make me feel better.'

'No. No, I'm not. I'm your team leader, Grace. I'm not here to make you feel better. I'm here to assess your work and make sure you're a good fit for the team.'

She bit her lip. She was waiting. Waiting for him to say she should go. He couldn't stand how upset she looked.

Grace Barclay really had no idea just how good she was.

He did something he probably shouldn't. He stroked a finger down her cheek. The lightest, gentlest touch against her soft, silky skin. It was a much more intimate gesture than before. 'Grace, I think you are very capable. You were in a situation that was unusual for you. You recognised that you hadn't handled a paediatric arrest and asked for assistance. Some people might not have done that. One of the biggest faults a doctor can have is not to recognise their own shortcomings. But you did brilliantly in there, Grace. You have no reason to doubt your abilities.'

Her lips were still quivering. Tears were shimmering in her eyes.

He lowered his lips to her ear. 'I don't.' It was a whisper. But he said it with the intensity he thought she was due.

He felt her suck in a breath and hold it. He straightened up and dropped a kiss on her head, pulling her close again. It felt natural. It felt like a completely natural response.

But they weren't the actions of a team leader. And he knew that.

She relaxed against him for a few seconds, her hands reaching down and touching the sides of his waist.

Then he moved and did something he absolutely shouldn't. He sat on the bed next to her and lay back, pulling her with him so she rested against his chest. His arms were encircling her warm body. He could still feel the shudders going through her. And he didn't say a single word.

What was he doing?

He'd never had a relationship with anyone in his team before. He'd never got this close to anyone in his team before.

But Grace was different. From those first few moments in the shower he'd known things were different.

Keeping her at arm's length was becoming more tricky. And he certainly didn't have her at arm's length right now. As soon as he'd realised how upset she was, he'd been unable to stop himself from putting his arms around her. He'd comforted lots of colleagues in the past by giving them a quick hug, but this was different.

Everything about Grace Barclay confused him. And part of him was hoping she was just as confused as he was.

The shuddering came to a peaceful end. He had one hand wrapped around her body and the other gently stroking her hair. It had seemed natural. He hadn't even thought to stop. Their breathing had slowly synched and he could almost feel the gradual change in the air around them.

The time for comforting had passed. He really didn't have an excuse to be lying on a bed with Grace Barclay now. But he didn't really want to move.

And it seemed that neither did she.

He could sense the change in her breathing again. The awareness.

Electricity seemed to be forming in the air above them.

He squeezed his eyes closed. What was he thinking? They had young patients to prepare for transfer out there. Grace had notes to write up. And his mind was somewhere else entirely. He felt another sensation, a rush of blood and a stirring awareness elsewhere.

Enough.

He sat up rapidly, pushing Grace up along with him. For a second she looked a little flustered and he prayed she hadn't noticed anything going on in his body.

He took a deep breath and tried to sound as professional as he could. 'Better?'

He stood up and made a grab for Tyler's notes, which he'd abandoned on a nearby chair.

She lifted her chin. She looked calmer now. More like herself. She licked her lips. 'Better.'

Neither of them were going to acknowledge what had just happened.

He tried to keep it all business. 'We need to write up Tyler's notes to prepare him for the transfer.'

She nodded. He had no idea what was going on in her head right now.

She reached out her hand. 'I'll do it. You wait for the medevac team.'

It was back to business. She took the notes and

pushed open the door. It let in a gust of fresh air that cooled the body parts that had been reacting and he watched her walk down the corridor to the nurses' station and start writing.

He smiled. She'd just given him an order.

And, team leader or not, he kind of liked it.

CHAPTER SIX

GRACE'S PHONE BEEPED as she turned on the shower in the slightly rundown motel room. The only saving grace of this place, with its old-fashioned décor and rough towels, was the fact it looked directly onto the beach.

She was trying to calculate in her head how long she'd been awake, but her brain was currently mush, so she'd reverted to using her fingers. She had been up since six-thirty yesterday morning, then a late-night flight, arrival in the Florida hospital after midnight, followed by a full eleven-hour shift. Callum Ferguson had arrived just under an hour ago and taken a full handover from every member of staff, then he had promptly sent them all to go and sleep.

Donovan hadn't wanted to leave. He'd been hanging around Callum like a moth to a flame. It was only natural. It had only been two years ago that Callum had experienced a heart attack on a DPA mission. Everyone was naturally protective of the man they all admired. But Grace had noticed there was an extra doctor in Callum's team. She could only guess he'd been placed there by the director to ensure Callum had enough support.

Eventually, Donovan had agreed to leave but only with a guarantee that if there was an influx of patients he be called back in.

She put her hand under the shower, shrieked and pulled it back. The water was icy cold. A bit like the water at the DPA when Donovan had turned the showers off.

She looked out of her window at the beach. Maybe there was an alternative? The sun wasn't even close to setting and there were still lots of people in the water. She opened her mammoth case and pulled out the orange bikini. Her friends must have had a sixth sense. She could put this to some use.

The phone beeped again and she picked it up. A text message from Lara.

Love you, honey, but you need to check out your Twitter feed.

She screwed up her face. What on earth did that mean? She tapped the app open and started to scroll down the last few hours of tweets. Her heart stopped and she held the phone closer to her face. Did it really say that?

Best way to get on a team? Get naked with the boss in a shower! #whosentthatmysteriouspack-age?

Her legs felt like wobbly jelly and she sagged onto the corner of the bed. She recognised who had sent the tweet. It was another member of staff at the DPA. Frank Parker had always been obnoxious in the extreme but this was a whole other level.

Her hands started to shake. The first part was hurtful. Sexist. Something that wasn't entirely unusual for Frank, whose ambition emanated from his very pores. He was obviously furious that she'd got the place on a team that he would have likely killed for.

But it was the hashtag that killed her. She took a deep breath. The upset shaking was stopping. It was being rapidly overtaken by trembling rage.

How dared he? He was implying that she'd had something to do with the package. That she had somehow manipulated things to trick her way onto a team.

It was pathetic. Truly and utterly pathetic. There was no conceivable way she could have predicted she would be opening mail that day—who on earth could switch on their telepathic powers to know someone else would be off sick? And who on earth could know that Donovan would have been the nearest team leader at that moment of time?

It was insulting, but it was also manipulative. Other members of staff at the DPA would have seen this. Why else would Lara have given her a heads-up?

She sent a quick text back, thanking Lara but containing a few expletives about Frank. She couldn't help it. If he'd appeared in her room right now she could have killed him with her bare hands.

She started pulling her clothes over her head, leaving them scattered over the floor. Normally Grace was a neat freak. But all those compulsions had left her. She switched off the still-cold shower. There was no way she was getting in there.

Her shoulder gave a little twinge as she fastened her bikini top. It was odd, almost as if her body occasionally came out in sympathy with her. She grabbed her flip-flops and slammed the door behind her.

She wasn't normally a beach bunny. She didn't have the figure or the inclination for it. But today the beach had never looked so good. She was sticky. She was uncomfortable. And maybe a quick dip in the ocean would wash away the horrible sensation that was creeping over her skin.

Or maybe it would help her plan her revenge…

Donovan was fretting. It didn't matter that Callum appeared to be back to full health and was working as a team leader again. It didn't matter that someone had decided to put an extra member on his team.

He was still worried. He loved the big guy. He admired him. He wanted to *be* him when he grew up. Most of the doctors at the DPA felt like about the Granddad of Disease. He couldn't imagine how sick to her stomach Callie Turner must have felt two years ago when Callum had had an MI on a flight with her. Which was why he had a horrible sinking feeling that he shouldn't have left the hospital.

That was the trouble with admiring someone so much. He didn't want Callum to think he was being disrespectful by hanging around. So now he would just have to make sure his phone was permanently charged in case of a call.

He heard a little yelp next door and gave a smile. He'd recognise that noise anywhere. Grace had obviously discovered the showers came from a mysterious underground water pump flowing directly from the Arctic. He'd tried to speak to the guy on the front desk about the cold water but he'd been on the phone and had just shrugged and gestured Donovan away.

He looked out at the blue ocean. Unsurprisingly there was no gym or workout room at this low-cost motel and Donovan thrived on his daily run. A jog along the beach would be perfect.

Even though he had an ocean view the walls in this smaller-than-average room felt as if they were pressing in around him. A sensation that didn't sit well with him. It didn't matter that it would be warmer outside than in. The air-conditioning in the room was clawing at his skin.

It was still light and the beach wasn't too busy at this time of the day. There were only a few die-hard surfers and some families that hadn't yet packed up for the day. He pulled on his running shorts and vest, tucking his cellphone in one pocket and his music player in the other. He could brave the cold shower later or, if the beach was quieter, he might even go for a swim.

It had been a long time since Donovan had run on sand. It didn't matter that he'd moved onto the firmer sand next to the shoreline. He could still feel his muscles burn. The late afternoon sun felt good on his shoulders, relaxing even. The sounds of Dire Straits pounded in his ears.

Atlanta was so different from here. No beaches. No view of the never-ending ocean. There were a few parks but none close to where Donovan lived. Just miles and miles of apartments and buildings. Street running just wasn't the same.

He could get used to this.

He glanced at his watch and slowed his speed. He averaged around three miles back home, listening to the same tracks. The beach was a little emptier now and he could feel the rivulets of sweat run down his back and chest. It had been years since he had gone swimming. Some of his friends had pools but they weren't designed for serious exercise—not like the kind Donovan craved. Time for a swim in the ocean.

There were no warning flags. No lifeguards either. But Donovan wasn't worried. He just wanted a chance to sluice off.

He ditched his running shoes and vest, putting his phone and MP3 player underneath the pile on the sand. It only took a few strides to reach the edge of the water.

He placed his hands on his hips and took a few deep breaths, arching his back to stretch out any lingering sore muscles. The water was chilly but not as cold as the shower.

As he took another few steps he could see a few people around him. A few hundred yards up the beach some surfers had gathered, half in the water and half out, watching the waves from under their hands as they shielded out the glare from the lowering sun.

A swimmer was coming back in, their smooth overhead strokes barely causing a ripple in the water around them. It was a woman and she slowed, obviously catching her feet on the sea-bed.

She moved closer as the water cascaded around her. Dark shoulder-length hair, a bright orange bikini and a curvaceous figure. Hadn't there been a scene like this in a James Bond movie?

His breath tightened in his throat as he realised who it was. Grace. Somehow he hadn't figured she'd prefer a dip in the ocean to the cold shower. Grace didn't seem like the type.

He walked towards her, the waves surrounding his hips and chest. The water was streaming down her face and she rubbed her eyes as she took the tough strides forward against the tide.

Her hands froze as Donovan came into focus. He didn't know where to put his gaze. It was automatically drawn to her breasts and hips in the orange bikini against her lightly tanned skin.

He'd already seen every part of Grace. But that didn't matter. That had been work. That had been professional—and it had been a clinical emergency.

Seeing Grace Barclay gliding out of the water towards him, barely dressed, with the gradually dipping sun glinting off her tanned skin, was a whole other ball game.

'Donovan.' The word came out a little breathless. A little throaty. She might just have been swimming towards him—it might have been entirely natural for her to be out of breath—but the timbre of her voice had a direct effect on his senses.

He moved towards her, drawn like a magnet. Walking against the tide until only a few inches of ocean water held them apart.

Their gazes met in open acknowledgement of

the sexual attraction between them. He could see the glimmer of nerves and uncertainty in her eyes. Why would Grace doubt he was attracted to her?

'Hey,' he murmured. He couldn't stop his eyes devouring her body. Looking made his hands tingle to reach and touch all parts of her. This close he could see a few tiny freckles scattered across the bridge of her nose. Had they just appeared?

He had a new appreciation of her shorter hairstyle. Now none of her body was shielded from his gaze. Everything was there for his appreciation. And, boy, did he appreciate it.

Grace wasn't acting too shy herself. 'Hey,' she replied, as her gaze focused on his broad chest. Donovan was used to working out. He liked to be fit. He liked to stay healthy. There was no spare fat on his body, just toned muscle. Her gaze followed the scattering of hair across his chest that darkened and increased as it drew her eyes downwards. It was almost teasing her to keep following its line across his flat abdomen and beyond.

No one else was near them. His peripheral vision was shutting out any movement or colour around them. All of his focus was on Grace. His internal monologue was trying to talk sense to him but right now he wasn't thinking about the fact she was a member of his team. Right now he was doing his best to forget it. Right now he was concentrating on the fact that every time he was near Grace his senses were scrambled. All he could think about was acting on the unspoken acknowledgement between them.

He smiled. He couldn't help it. It was a smile of expectation about what could happen next.

The sun was getting lower in the sky behind her, lighting up every curve of her body, every drop of water on her skin. He couldn't have pictured her any more perfectly.

The tidal surges were strong. They were hit by one wave and dragged back towards the ocean by another. His reactions were automatic and his hands were on her waist in an instant. Her palms landed on his chest and they both lowered their gazes, staring at them there.

Her eyes lifted to meet his. The green almost hidden next to her wide dark pupils. He could see the pulse throbbing at the base of her neck and it willed him to lean a little closer. To touch it with his mouth.

'Great minds think alike,' he murmured. He was talking about the fact they'd both headed for the ocean. But it didn't quite come out like that. Not while they were standing so close and their bodies were touching. It was as if the words danced across her skin, edging her closer until their hips met underwater. The cool water was doing nothing to dull the fire in his blood. Nothing to dampen his desire for her. If things heated up any more the ocean around them would start to sizzle.

His fingers around her waist pulled her even closer, leaving her in no shadow of a doubt about his reaction to her bikini-clad body.

Her body reacted too, her nipples hardening against his chest.

This was it. This was the outcome of the electricity that had been around them right from the start. If Donovan stuck his hand into a socket right now he could light up the national grid.

He felt her take a deep breath. It was as if she were calming herself. Steadying herself for the next step. She relaxed her head and neck, letting her head tip back to reveal the pale skin of her throat. Her hands moved, sliding slowly up his chest onto his shoulders, and he let out an involuntary groan. She raised herself on tiptoe under the water, bringing her head into closer alignment to his. He tipped his downwards until their noses almost touched.

Neither had really spoken. Only those few words. But the air around them was charged with electricity. Every time she breathed her barely covered breasts came into contact with the planes of his chest.

Donovan didn't want to waste another second. He dipped his head and claimed her lips as his own, tasting the salt, mixed with some lip balm. Her arms curled around his neck as she pressed her body into his. Grace wasn't shy. She was more than a match for his kisses.

Their mouths parted and the kiss deepened. His hands moved from her waist, sliding down the curve of her firm backside. Her breasts were pressed against his chest. Grace Barclay was all woman. And, boy, did it turn him on.

There was a little noise. A little whimper as their kiss deepened. Heat was coursing through his body. He moved from her full lips, turning his attention to the soft skin of her neck and throat. Finding the throbbing pulse at the nape of her neck and luxuriating in her sighs as he worked his way round.

His hand moved in one movement from outside of her bikini bottom to the inside, cupping the bare skin of her backside. No one was close enough to see a thing, and even if they had been, the ocean was covering the lower halves of their bodies.

Her fingers were gliding across his back, pulling him even closer as they were buffeted by the waves. Then they changed direction, following his lead downwards. The movement made his stomach muscles twitch as they skirted past the hairs on his lower abdomen and headed even lower. They skirted around the edges of his shorts, tentatively making their way beneath.

Suddenly this seemed like a much more private party.

He let out a growl and pulled back. Her eyes

widened at his release and the water swept between them. He lifted his feet from the sea bed, leaning back a little and letting the water take his weight. Grace was breathing heavily, trying to compose herself after what had just happened. Donovan was hoping the cool water would soothe the fire in his groin. Thank goodness for baggy running shorts. Leaving the water could give someone an eyeful.

Her breathing started to slow. He could see the hesitation flickering in her eyes. There it was again. That doubt.

Why did she think he'd stopped? He'd had to. They were on a public beach. It was the first time he'd touched her. The time in the DPA shower had been entirely different. He wasn't even sure what he was doing here. He'd never made a move on a colleague before.

Relationships in the DPA had consequences.

He moved in the water, catching her hand in his. 'Grace? We're out in the open. Anyone could see us.'

'I know.' Her voice was quiet. She straightened as her feet connected with the sea bed again and she took a couple of steps closer to the shore. Her eyes were averted, focusing on the motel next to the beach. 'This wasn't meant to happen.'

The words jolted him from the current euphoria his body was feeling. It was one thing for him to have doubts about what he was doing. It was another for Grace. Was he really that arrogant? He planted his feet down. A wave of disquiet started to crowd his senses. Maybe he'd misread this situation completely. 'What do you mean?'

Her voice had the tiniest tremble, but her tone was determined. 'I mean that you're my boss. This is my first assignment.'

She was saying the words, but the conviction in her eyes just wasn't there. His head started to swim. What was he doing? Law suits and legal terms started to circulate in his brain. Would Grace claim some kind of harassment? The cool breeze prickled his skin, every hair on his arms standing on end. He had no idea how to play this. He'd never been involved with someone at work before. Had never wanted to cross that line. Maybe this was why.

'Are you trying to deny what's happening between us, Grace? Tell me I'm not imagining this. Tell me I'm not reading this wrong.' He was feeling panicked. Was all of this in his head? He'd never had any problems reading signals from the opposite sex before. The thought that he'd misread Grace was alarming in more ways than one.

But Grace shook her head. There was a sheen in her eyes. Was she going to cry?

He reached over before he could stop himself, putting his hands on her shoulders. 'Then what is it, Grace? Tell me what's wrong.'

He could see her gulp, licking her lips and flinching from the taste of salt that must be on them. The tremble in her voice had increased. 'Go online, Donovan. Read Twitter. See what my colleagues have to say about me.' She pressed her hand to her chest. 'I want people to think I earned my place on the team not by getting naked with the boss. I want to be here because I deserve to be here. Not because you've decided I'm flavour of the month.'

'What on earth are you talking about?' She was moving away. Striding back towards the shoreline.

He couldn't figure out what was going on here. One minute she had been kissing him like her life depended on it, the next she'd been looking at him as if he'd just crossed some unspeakable line. Which he had. And which he didn't want to think about.

The semantics of should he/shouldn't he kiss a team member couldn't even figure in his brain right now. What was front and centre was the way Grace had just looked at him. As if she'd been disgusted with both him and herself. As if they'd just done something terrible.

That was the expression that was going to keep him awake tonight.

'Grace! Come back. Talk to me.' His voice verged on desperation. He almost didn't recognise the sound. None of this was familiar to him.

But his words fell on deaf ears. Her strides were becoming longer as she neared the shore and the pull of the water lessened.

Should he go after her?

If she'd been wearing anything else when she'd come down here it was clear she was abandoning it. As she hit the beach she didn't stop, walking as swiftly as possible across the sand and back to the motel.

He had a clear view of her body, but his eyes were drawn to the ragged scar on her shoulder. In this fading light it stood out angry and red. A clear reminder of something that had happened in Grace's past. Something he didn't know about. Something he wanted to ask her about.

Every bone in his body wanted to go after her. But every brain cell told him not to.

He had to stop. He had to think this through. What on earth did she mean about Twitter—and why would that have any impact on what was happening between them?

Donovan couldn't remember the last time he'd logged onto his account. Social media wasn't really his thing. He liked the internet, he liked the opportunity of access to information and facts whenever he needed it. But did he really want to know what someone else had for dinner? No. Not at all.

A wave rolled over his head and shoulders, pushing him towards the shore. The momentum gave him some motivation to move. Slowly.

It would be so easy to power up the beach after her. But Donovan was normally known for his self-control. The incident with the gun had proved that. He walked out of the water, grabbing his vest in his hands and checking his phone.

No messages. No calls from Callum.

He was about to look away when he remembered the app. He clicked on the Twitter button. The last time he'd looked had been thirty-five days ago. Showed how often he paid attention to it.

The phone almost shook in protest and the data downloaded. He started scrolling, letting his still-wet fingers drip water onto the screen. Nothing. Nothing. Nothing.

He followed a number of colleagues at work, some national Twitter feeds about public health, and some official organisations. His feed wasn't exactly overrun with celebrity small talk.

Then his finger froze and he squinted at the screen. He expanded the words with his fingers. No way. Frank Parker. That little no-good stinking rat.

Donovan had never liked him. Too cocky. Too

confident. That would be fine if he had the kudos to go along with it. But he didn't. Donovan had picked him up a few times on clinical errors and not following protocols.

He could feel the heat surge into his cheeks. Fury building in his chest. He'd kill him. He'd kill him and drag his body off to some dark forest somewhere.

He could hide a body. He could do that. He'd watched *CSI* enough times to know about forensic evidence. Or maybe he could poison the creep. Better still, he could just wring his neck with his bare hands.

He couldn't remember the last time he'd felt rage like this.

He stopped on the sand, hand on his hip, and took a few deep breaths, trying to still the fury and uncontrollable thoughts. No wonder Grace was upset. No wonder the last thing she wanted to be seen doing was kissing the boss.

The implications were clear.

But Frank Parker couldn't be more wrong if he'd tried. He and Grace had never had a conversation before the incident. They had no relationship. And Grace was incapable of anything he'd accused her of.

As for the implied slur on him—that he'd selected Grace for anything other than her expertise—that did make him mad.

The caveman urges started to dissipate and the DPA team leader's mind started to reappear. This was unprofessional conduct without a shadow of a doubt. A phone call to the director was called for. His legs started covering the beach in long strides.

He had worked hard for this position. He wasn't about to let some trouble-making colleague call his professionalism into question.

Yes. He had given Grace the job without application or interview, but that wasn't unusual in the DPA. As soon as a team member revealed she was pregnant she was immediately pulled from fieldwork. It was a necessity.

If it had been a few weeks before the team was called out again, he would have time to interview from the pool of potential candidates already within the DPA. Their recruitment for fieldwork teams was always done internally.

But because they had been called out straight away he'd had to make the decision to select a new team member or leave with a member down. People had been recruited like this before. Grace had impressed him with her knowledge and expertise. She was ready. She was ready for a fieldwork assignment.

Frank Parker was not. His skills were best suited to the lab.

His phone buzzed. A text. From Callum Ferguson.

Just heard about the social media debacle. Frank Parker will never have a place on my team or yours. Tell Grace I think she's done a stellar job so far. As for you, keep calm. The damage is done. Talk to the Director. Tell him if Frank Parker is still in the office when I return I'll deal with him myself.

A smile spread across his face. It wasn't just him that was about to blow a gasket. There was reassurance from the Granddad of Disease that he thought Frank's actions were inappropriate too. The big Scotsman always spoke his mind and took no prisoners. Donovan shook his head. He would speak to the director. And he would pass on Callum's warning. Neither he, nor the director, would want to see Callum's reaction.

He scrolled down for the number of the director's PA. The phone answered after two rings.

'DPA, Director Kane's office.'

'Julie? It's Donovan Reid. Can I speak to the director?'

There was a long pause. 'Yes, Donovan. We were expecting your call. Unfortunately Director Kane is unavailable.'

'I need to talk to him as soon as possible.'

He could almost hear the smile in her voice. 'He's dealing with a member of staff who is being transferred to another office immediately. I'm doing the paperwork now.'

Donovan pulled back his shoulders. The inference was there. 'Is it who I think it is?'

Julie cleared her throat, 'Let's just say the same individual will have a permanent note regarding unprofessional conduct and bringing the organisation into disrepute on their file.'

'I don't need to call back, do I, Julie?'

'I wouldn't think so. The director is keen for his fieldwork teams to be able to concentrate on the job in hand.'

'No problem.' He cut the call. It was strange what a surge of pleasure he felt at hearing those few words. Someone had obviously alerted the director to the comment in the social media and he'd acted immediately. Just the way he should.

He reached the entrance to the motel. He had to let Grace know things had been dealt with. She didn't need to think about Frank Parker's comments. She didn't need to think about what had just happened on the beach. She could just concentrate on being Grace Barclay, doctor on her first fieldwork assignment.

He was outside her door a few moments later, his hand hesitating for a second before he knocked on the door. He had to keep this professional. He had to keep this above board.

He stood in silence for a few moments. Was Grace not going to answer the door? Maybe she'd looked through the peephole and decided not to answer? He didn't even want to admit how much those thoughts bothered him. How very uncomfortable they made him.

The door inched open, Grace's face appearing in the narrow gap. Her hair was bundled up on her head and one of the thin motel towels was wrapped around her body.

'You braved the ice-cold shower?' He said the first thing that came to mind and wanted to grab the words back as soon as he'd said them. Of course she'd had a shower. Anything to cool the heat that had been in their bodies.

She adjusted the towel, trying to cover her boobs a little more. 'I didn't have much choice.' She said the words quietly. 'What do you want, Donovan?'

He glanced over his shoulder. He really didn't want to have this conversation in the corridor. 'Can I come in?' When her face didn't change he added, 'It's about work.'

It felt strange, having to talk his way into a woman's room. He'd never had to do that in his life before. He'd never wanted to do it before. But this was different. This was important.

She gave a brief nod then opened the door, allowing him to edge inside.

The room felt oppressive. Dark and closed in. He almost didn't want her to close the door behind him. He was conscious of how close he was to her and kept his arms firmly by his sides. Resisting the urge to reach out and touch her.

'Grace, I called the office.'

Her eyes were huge in the dim room. Her pupils dark and wide. She was biting her bottom lip, obviously nervous. 'What did they say?'

'I didn't even get to speak to the director. I suspect he had Frank in his office and was tearing a few strips off him. He's being transferred to another office.'

Her eyes widened. 'Really? Just like that?' She took a few seconds then stared down at the floor. Her voice was quiet. 'All because of one tweet?'

'Don't you dare feel sorry for him, Grace.' He kept his voice low. He hated the way she looked right now. Hated it that she'd been hurt. Grace had no idea what people really thought of her. Her confidence had been shattered by Frank Parker's one selfish act. He pulled his phone from his pocket and held it out towards her. 'Read this.'

'What is it?' Her hand reached out hesitantly before she took the phone and pressed the button to light up the screen. It only took her a few seconds to read the message. Her hand came up to her mouth. 'Oh. Wow. Callum Ferguson said that about me?'

He nodded. There was an edge of disbelief to her voice and her expression was changing. All in an instant. Her shoulders and back straightened, making her two inches taller. Her eyes lit up and the corners of her lips curved upwards. It was like she'd just been given a shot of confidence. And the transformation was startling.

'Yes, Callum Ferguson said that about you.' It would be so easy to cross the small space between them and put his arms around her. But he wouldn't do it. Not again.

Not unless she asked him to.

He had to keep this on a professional footing. For both their sakes.

He put his hand on the doorhandle. Even with Grace lit up he still didn't like this small space.

At this rate he would spend the night sleeping with the doors in his room open to the beach.

'Why do you think I picked you for the team, Grace? Do you think for a single second it had anything to do with us ending up in the shower together?'

Her eyes widened slightly, probably in shock at the directness of his question.

She didn't answer straight away. Did that mean she was even considering it? Or that she was trying to conjure up another answer?'

Finally, she shook her head. 'I hope not.' Her voice was quiet, almost whispered. Her chin tilted upwards as she adjusted her towel again, drawing his gaze. 'I hope you picked me because I impressed you with my knowledge of the disease and not with my breast size.'

Her cheeks were flushed, as if she was embarrassed by the very thought of that.

He looked her straight in the eye. 'I'd already pulled your file, Grace, along with ten other candidates who would be suitable replacements for Mhairi Spencer on the team. You had glowing references from several of your previous placements in the DPA. Being exposed to the powder just brought us together a little quicker. We would have crossed paths soon.'

He folded his arms across his chest.

She stayed silent for a few seconds then sat on edge of the thin mattress on her bed. 'Thank you, Donovan. That means a lot. When I saw what had been written about me…it just made me doubt the reasons I was here.' She gave a rueful kind of smile. 'But I should have known better. After all, let's face it, I'm not exactly your type, am I?'

Her tone had changed. They were back to the informal, almost playful mood that bounced between them.

He tilted his head to the side. 'My type? What is that?'

He was amused.

She looked down at her body covered in the thin towel. 'I'm hardly your usual. Don't you usually date tall, blonde, willowy types?'

'Do I?'

'Apparently.'

'And are they my type?' He was still amused.

He wasn't aware that he only dated one kind of woman.

She shrugged. 'So I've heard.'

'I had no idea my love life was of interest to my colleagues at the DPA. That's why I never date at work. Too many complications. I don't like anything interfering with the job.'

Her brow furrowed. 'Why is that?' Straight to the point. He was getting to learn that this was a trait of Grace's. And, to be honest, it was part of her appeal. He'd never liked tiptoeing around people before. It was much better to be up front. Yeah, well. About most things.

'I like my work to be about work. I don't like distractions at work. I had a colleague who once got distracted when his wife was taken ill. It played havoc with our work.'

It was almost like a cold chill passed over her body, even though she knew the air temperature hadn't changed. 'You're talking about Matt Sawyer's first wife, aren't you? She died on a mission a few years ago.'

His feet shifted uncomfortably and his tanned face had a pale look. Everyone knew about the mission. Everyone knew that Matt had disappeared off the grid for a number of years after that. No one had known if he was dead or alive. Not until he'd turned up two years ago in Chicago with a suspected smallpox outbreak. After a rocky start he'd hit it off with Callie Turner, the doctor who'd led the investigation team. They were married now, with a toddler son, and Sawyer was working with the DPA again on the lecturing circuit.

Donovan looked uncomfortable. 'That was my first fieldwork assignment.'

'You were there when she died?'

He took a hesitant breath. 'Yes…it was awful. He held her in his arms for hours. There was absolutely nothing we could do. Nothing at all. I watched him fall to pieces. All because his wife had been on that fieldwork assignment with him.'

She lifted her hands, conscious that her thin towel was edging downwards. 'But that was a one-off. Nothing like that has happened since. Matt's moved on now. He's married with a kid. So are his sister Violet and Evan Hunter.

They met at work too. Why do you think it's such an issue?'

'Because I was there, Grace. I saw someone who was one of the best doctors I'd ever worked with unravel at the seams. And look at your examples. Callie doesn't work for the DPA any more and neither does Violet. They all realised that having an emotional attachment at work means you can't always do the job you should.'

She took a few steps towards him. She was feeling more and more at ease in his company. It wasn't that any other guy had ever threatened her. But since the attack, being alone in one place with a guy was a big deal for her. Particularly in the fast-fading light.

Being around Donovan wasn't uncomfortable. Maybe she was still aware of the touch of his skin, the feel of his lips. Maybe it was the satisfaction of the electricity that seemed to sizzle in the air between them. Whatever it was, it was the first time in a long time she'd been totally at ease—even in her current state of undress.

'I don't agree, Donovan.' She laid her hand on his forearm. 'I only know what I've heard through the grapevine. I heard that Callie Turner hadn't really wanted to work in this line anyway. And Violet? She's moved to specialise in foetal alcohol syndrome. I'm not sure the change of jobs was anything to do with working with their husbands.'

He frowned. 'Do you think you could have a relationship at work and be impartial to the job? Do you really think you could be unemotionally attached if something happened to someone you loved?'

She shrugged her shoulders. 'I don't know. I've never thought about it.' She met his gaze. 'I've never had reason to.' She paused for a second, not believing she'd just said that out loud.

'That's why you don't date anyone from work? Really?' She shook her head and leaned against the wall. 'I love my job, Donovan. I do. I've no idea which part of the DPA I'll end up in. But I do know that I would love my partner to share my enthusiasm and commitment to the job. It's hard to explain to someone else that you have to fly away at a moment's notice and you can't give any indication of when you'll be back. How do you get someone—who doesn't understand our work—to understand that?'

He was watching her closely and as his face softened she wondered if it sounded as if she was trying to persuade him he should be dating her. Her words might have implied that and the thought made her cringe. She didn't want to have to persuade someone to be interested in her. That was embarrassing.

There was the tiniest shake of his head. The muscles in his body tensed. But his voice was quiet. Resolute. 'I don't date colleagues, Grace.'

There was no doubt where that was aimed. But instead of hurting her, it only made her indignant.

This time she didn't reach out gently and touch his forearm. This time she stepped right up to his chest, her head directly underneath his. 'So you just kiss them, then?'

It was the fewest of words. With everything implied.

She had no idea what was going on his head or hers. She'd been swept away when he'd kissed her.

They couldn't deny the attraction between them any more—not when they'd both acted on it.

Kissing the boss was never an ideal situation. And she didn't want people to second-guess why she'd got the job.

But part of her was curious about her feelings towards Donovan. She'd never felt a buzz like this before. But in the last few months she'd never met anyone she felt safe around either. Donovan was both.

The dim light cast a shadow over his face. For a few seconds she didn't know whether he was angry or sad. She could almost read his scrambled thoughts as he tried to make sense of her reasoning.

His fingers clenched around the door handle behind him. He was going to leave. He was going to walk away.

But he didn't. He dropped his lips to hers as her towel slipped to the floor and all rational thought left the building.

Her lips tasted even sweeter than before, the feel of her naked body next to his igniting all his senses. One hand circled his back, her palm stroking up and down the length of his spine. The other lifted to the side of his cheek and her fingers scraped against the feel of his stubble.

Remember why you're here. The words echoed in his brain as his scrambled senses tried to make order of what he was doing. Grace was beautiful. Utterly delectable.

She was making him lose focus. Making him lose sight of his goals. He was here to do a good job. To get to the bottom of the Marburg virus outbreak. People were already talking. Grace was already under the microscope.

It would hardly ingratiate him or her to the director if he suspected anything had happened between them.

He pulled away, breaking their kiss suddenly. Her lips were reddened and full, her breathing heavy. She was startled and it was hardly surprising. She was standing naked in front of him and if he stayed there a minute longer he would never leave.

He put his hand back on the doorhandle. 'I'm

sorry, Grace. I have to go. This can't happen between us.'

He yanked the door open and strode out into the warm Florida air before he changed his mind.

CHAPTER SEVEN

SHE WAS WALKING down the corridor towards him in a purple wraparound dress, flat shoes and her white coat. But in Donovan's head she was wearing that orange bikini again and walking out from the sun-kissed ocean with water streaming from her body.

'Donovan? Did you hear me?' A pointed elbow stuck into his ribs.

'Hey!' He turned. John was looking at him with an amused expression on his face. His eyes drifted off towards Grace, who'd stopped to speak to one of the nurses in the corridor.

John raised his eyebrows. 'If I could manage to keep your attention, even for a few minutes, that would be great.'

He felt a rush of colour to his cheeks. When was the last time he'd actually blushed? Embarrassment wasn't the norm for him. Then again, he'd always been completely focused on the job before. After the events of last night he was wondering if he'd ever be able to focus on the job again.

He'd been right. This was why getting involved with someone at work was a bad idea. A really bad idea.

He pulled himself back into professional mode. 'What's up, John?'

John held out the paperwork in his hands towards him. 'After fighting for two days, I've finally managed to secure us entry to the national park.'

Donovan smiled and nodded. 'You mean after two days of careful negotiations.'

John let out a stream of colourful language. 'No. I mean fighting.'

'So we're in?'

'We're in. You can collect the samples this afternoon.'

The words flowed over him and every sense on his body went on full alert. 'Aren't you collecting the samples?'

John shook his head. 'Callum asked if I could

help out in the lab once the case histories were investigated. The samples are practically meeting David at the door right now.'

Donovan bit the inside of his cheek. Darn it. He wasn't going to countermand an order given by Callum. He might have been the first team leader on the job, but now Callum was here the final decisions would really be made by him.

He cleared his throat. Maybe this wouldn't be as bad as he was expecting. 'Where exactly are we collecting the samples from?'

John checked his reference sheets. 'The fruit bats have some nests in the surrounding tree trunks, but their primary habitat is in the limestone caves. There is a tour of the caves and the entrance and walkways are lit up. Unfortunately, there's no lighting further inside where the bats roost.'

The horrible creeping sensation he'd been expecting washed over his body. He didn't care about lights. What he did care about was an open exit route.

'How far into the caves do we need to go?'

John shook his head. 'I'm not sure. I think it

might be around eight hundred metres. I can check if you want?'

'No. That's fine.'

Eight hundred metres. Half a mile. Well away from any visible entrance point. Tracks in caves didn't go in nice straight lines. Not like Roman roads. No, they would follow every twist and turn of the mountain they were worn into.

John looked back down the corridor and smiled. It was obvious he was oblivious to the thoughts currently crowding Donovan's head. 'I take it you'll want to take our newest recruit on the sample-collecting expedition?'

His head jerked round. Did John know something had gone on between them? How could he?

He bit back the snappy reply that was about to form on his lips. He'd worked with this guy for three years. John was older, and maybe a whole lot wiser. It was obvious he was just yanking his chain. And he had nobody to blame but himself. John had obviously noticed the way he was looking at Grace.

That would have to stop.

'Grace!' he shouted down the corridor, his tone a bit sharper than he'd actually meant it to be.

She started and turned round. For a second her eyes widened as she caught the expression on his face, then she obviously realised John was by his side. Her feet moved quickly down the corridor and he willed himself not to watch the swing of her hips in that confounded dress. Her clothes—or lack of them—were going to be the death of him.

'I've reviewed most of the patients,' she started quickly. 'There are a few who need some further attention, but most are stable for the moment.'

She was doing exactly what he would expect her to do. Getting on with the job. But even the way she said those words crept under his skin. The quick talking was obviously a self-defence mechanism. He recognised it, because he was in that place himself.

John seemed oblivious. 'Looks like you've got a state park to visit.'

He held the paperwork up to her and her eyes scanned the page. Her fingers automatically moved to her hair, grabbing a little strand and twisting it round one index finger. He noticed the tiniest, subtlest widening of her eyes. 'I'm going to collect the samples?' Was that the smallest tremor in her voice?

John kept smiling. He didn't notice all the little nuances in Grace's behaviour that Donovan did. 'Yeah, you and Donovan are going this afternoon.'

'Can't you go?' Her voice had risen in pitch and her eyes were fixed on John, almost as if she didn't want to look at Donovan in case he questioned her reaction. She hunched and then shrugged her shoulders, as if something had just irritated them.

Her scar. He hadn't asked her about the scar last night—even though he'd wanted to.

The smile had vanished from John's face. He reached up and touched Grace's arm. 'It's part of the initiation when you join a fieldwork team. You try out all roles in the team to see where you fit best. Would you prefer not to do it, Grace? Is there a problem?'

His voice was serious, questioning with a little hint of concern. It was important that every member of the team was able to function fully—filling in for each other in case of emergency. Grace had proved herself more than capable of dealing with the clinical cases, but the DPA fulfilled many more roles than that.

She was hesitating. The look on her face told him she was searching her brain for an appropriate answer. She fixed a smile on her face. 'No, John, it's fine.' Her eyes skimmed the information in front of her. 'We'll have guides, won't we? And the caves are lit?' There was an anxious tone to her voice, along with an edge of hopefulness.

Donovan was curious. She was asking the same kind of questions that he had. He hadn't noticed her having any kind of reaction in the isolation chamber back at the DPA. Enclosed spaces hadn't seemed to be an issue for her. So why the reluctance?

John's eyes were flicking between them both. He was obviously looking for a steer from Donovan. He spoke smoothly. 'I was just telling Donovan, the caves are quite deep and the fruit bats supposedly roost near the back of the caves. That's where you'll be collecting samples. The front part of the caves are lit for visitors, but not the back.'

She baulked. There was no other word for it.

John tried to fill the silence. 'They're supposed to be quite atmospheric. You know, with stalactites, stalagmites and lots of fossils. The cave tours are really popular.'

It was all sounding a bit desperado now. Donovan had no idea what her issue was. But he had issues of his own.

He lifted the paperwork from John's hands. 'Thanks for this. Grace, I'll meet you at the front entrance at one p.m.'

The abrupt words made her flinch. And the hurt expression on her face made him flinch in turn.

He couldn't afford to give her special treatment. He couldn't afford to make obvious allowances for her. She was expected to do a job. Just like he was.

He turned on his heel and walked away.

Right now she needed a good old-fashioned shot of midazolam. Something to sedate her and calm her down to a mild panic.

Florida, in summer, in a hazmat suit was not a good place. The suit was airtight, with a one-piece jumpsuit underneath and an outer suit impermeable to most chemicals. The sealed hood with its viewport was stifling, even though she had her own air supply, and the protective gloves made her feel like she had no dexterity at all.

The suits were a necessary evil. The route of exposure of the Marburg virus from the fruit bats had never been discovered. They knew how the virus passed from human to human, but how the virus had got into humans in the first place was still open to debate. It could be airborne, through contact with body fluids from the bats, or from surfaces in the caves. Therefore all staff had to wear protective, airtight suits. Nothing else was an option. They couldn't risk any more people being exposed to the virus.

She turned. There was no point moving just her head as the hood stayed in place and she ended up looking at the inside. She had to move her whole body round by shuffling her feet in the protective boots. Sweat was already beginning to pool on her forehead and she wasn't sure if it was the fact that the environment within the suit could be up to twenty or thirty degrees hotter than the temperature outside, or if it was the thought of going into those dark, imposing caves. As soon as the suit was sealed the humidity went up to one hundred per cent within a few minutes—not comfortable for any human.

People were assembling around her. The box for transporting the samples they would retrieve from the caves was sitting in front of her. She could hear Donovan talking through the speaker in the hood to those around about him.

The words were the slightest bit distorted, coming through the hood. But was that a trace of anxiety she could hear?

Grace tried some deep breathing. Long, slow breaths in and out. Her skin was prickling at the deep, blackness at the back of those caves. There was some lighting around the front, but the tourist part only lay in the front part of the caves. Where they were going was *waaaaayyy* back.

She shifted on her feet. She wanted to get this over and done with. If she'd known Donovan would keep talking for so long she would never have let them seal her suit. It was time for some definitive action. She picked up the kit box. 'Are we ready?'

Donovan's eyes met hers. There was something about wearing these suits. Lumbering around as if they were about to take a space-walk. There was layer upon layer within these suits and it almost felt as if they were separated by miles instead of inches.

The sun was reflecting off the faceplate of his sealed hood, making it hard to pick up any visual cues. But Donovan wasn't acting the way he normally did. He was saying twenty words when four would do.

It was almost as if he was stalling.

But why?

He'd looked at the plans for these caves. Four hundred metres in and they would have to turn a corner, following the natural line of the cave. Four hundred metres in and he would lose sight of the exit. He didn't care about how dark it was. He didn't care about how deep they went.

He just wished the way out was always visible.

Always in his line of sight. If it was, he would be fine. He could do this. But the map had already told them that wouldn't be possible.

Which was why he was currently using every delaying tactic under the sun. He hated this. He hated it that he felt like this.

This was the first time his childhood phobia was actually going to cause a problem for his job.

Over the last few years he'd always managed to hide his fear, control it even. The isolation chamber had been tough, but in his head he had always imagined the exit route. But the caves were unfamiliar. They weren't so easy to visualise.

The state ranger was beginning to look annoyed. And no wonder. A few beads of perspiration were already winding down his back—and he was used to wearing a hazmat suit. The poor guy must feel as if he were boiling alive.

He glanced over at the dark caves once again. It was almost as if they were mocking him, laughing at him and his juvenile fears.

This wasn't a sealed-in elevator with a door that might never open. Prickles started along his arms, running down to the palms of his hands.

It was like a million little centipedes stamping over his skin. He kept talking to himself. Willing himself to stay calm.

He had control. He was choosing to walk in there. He was the team leader. He had to collect these samples and establish if this was the cause of the outbreak. He had responsibilities, to himself and to his team.

And to Grace. She was shuffling around next to him as if someone had put itching powder in her suit. She'd never done this before. He had to set a good example for her.

He had to do this. The quicker he went in there the quicker he got out.

There. He'd convinced himself.

Grace had picked up the sample box and was hovering.

'Let's go, people.' He moved quickly before he changed his mind, walking as best he could in the uncomfortable suit. Grace and the state ranger quickly followed, but he was so focused, so intent on his goal that he barely noticed.

In and out. In and out. If he kept saying it, he might believe it.

* * *

Grace was doing her breathing exercises. She was clutching the sample box as if her life depended on it. What she really wanted to do was turn on her heel and run but, perhaps thankfully, her clumsy suit didn't allow for that.

She felt as if the blackness from the caves was reaching out towards her like a giant black hand, crossing over the pathways drenched in Florida sunlight and trying to envelop her and suck her in. It put her nerves on edge.

There was a bright white spotlight near the cave entrance, with another few lighting up some of the internal walkways. Her steps slowed as she neared the entry point. Her throat was dry and scratchy even though she'd taken a drink just before she'd been sealed into the suit. Any more liquid could result in other problems. What went in had to come out and she had no idea how long they would be in these caves.

She swallowed. The lights were fine, but they only focused on the front area. The state ranger was already heading through the first cave. Why did the fruit bats have to roost so far into the caves? Sadistic little critters.

She squeezed her eyes shut for a second—it was easier not to look—and walked straight into the back of Donovan. The face plate bashed against her nose. 'Ouch!'

Donovan turned round. He had the strangest expression on his face. 'What's wrong?' His voice was snappy and sounded even stranger as it came through the speaker and echoed around the cave.

'I…I…' Her brain wouldn't work. She couldn't figure out the words she wanted to say. The last thing she wanted to do was tell Donovan she was scared of the dark. It made her sound like a five-year-old.

Already the hairs were standing up on the back of her neck. The lights didn't reach around the corner they were about to turn and the shadows around her were disappearing rapidly.

It took a few minutes to realise that Donovan hadn't moved. His feet seemed just as stuck to the floor as hers.

'Hey!' The call came from the state ranger, who

hadn't wasted any time reaching the back area of the caves. 'Are you two coming?'

She gulped. Was she? Her hand reached up automatically to catch a lock of her hair and wind it around her finger. Impossible. Layer and layers were in the way.

Donovan's face changed. Was that a hint of a smile? Followed by a nervous laugh?

Her shoulder was itching uncontrollably. She had absolutely no chance of being able to scratch. She turned her back to the wall of the cave and pressed herself against it, trying to avoid the lumpy oxygen supply strapped inside her suit, while rubbing gently on the wall.

He was looking at her oddly.

She took a deep breath. 'I'm not good with caves.' Her eyes skirted around her surroundings. She was trying not to let her feelings envelop her. 'I'm not good with being in the dark. I was attacked a few years ago in a dark parking lot. Ever since then I've slept with the light on.' The words rushed out of her mouth before she could stop them. She didn't want to look at him. She didn't want to see the disappointment on his face.

Silence. All she could hear was her own breathing. Then one word came out of the darkness. The one she least expected.

'Snap.'

This was the worst feeling in the world. He'd never felt so exposed as he did right now.

Trouble was, Grace's expression was pretty much mirroring his own right now—and it wasn't because she was reflecting off his plastic hood.

He reached out and touched her shoulder. 'Do you want to leave, Grace?'

He was the team leader. He had to ask the question. He had to look out for his staff member. To be honest, if she said she wanted to leave right now it would give him an excuse to leave too.

The thought of having a panic attack around his colleagues was more than he could bear. But the prickling feeling on his skin, thudding heartbeats and rapid breathing couldn't really be anything else.

But he couldn't think about himself right now.

His own sensations of panic were being overtaken by a whole load of rage. 'Is that what the scar is on your shoulder?'

He flicked on the torch he had in his other hand. The darkness hadn't bothered him at all. He'd had the flashlight but just hadn't flicked the switch. He'd been too busy focusing on the entrance to the caves that was about to disappear from his line of sight.

The cave around them was illuminated in the light from the torch. There was a tear rolling down her cheek. His hand lifted to her visor. Too many layers, too many things in the way. All he wanted to do right now was wipe away her tear with his finger.

'You were stabbed in the attack?'

She nodded. He wanted to hold her. He wanted to wrap his arms around her and pull her close to his chest. The feelings were overwhelming. He'd known from the second he'd seen the angry scar that there must be a story behind it. He just hadn't banked on his reaction to that story.

He bent his knees so he was face to face with her. 'What were you doing in a dark parking lot at night, Grace? And why didn't you just give them your bag? It was only a bag. Things can be replaced. You can't.'

As he said the words he almost felt a hand around his heart, squeezing tightly. He hated the thought of someone doing that to her. He couldn't stand the fact she'd been attacked, let alone what outcome there could have been.

Her voice was shaky. 'I was working, Donovan. It was my last shift at Atlanta Park Hospital. I stayed a bit later to make sure my charts were up to date and by the time I got outside the lights were out in the parking lot.' She shook her head. 'I didn't fight him. I'm not that stupid. But he didn't care. He made a grab for my bag and just stabbed me anyway.'

He could see her whole body trembling inside the thick suit. 'That's why I don't like the dark. I get nervous. I have trouble dating now. I hate being alone with a man. It brings back a whole lot of memories I can't deal with. It doesn't matter that it's irrational. I know that. They're just still there.'

The dating stuff started circling around his

brain. Grace was nervous around men? Why hadn't he noticed? He'd kissed her, for goodness' sake!

But it was the other words that struck a chord. The irrational fears. They resounded around his head. 'I can relate to that, Grace.'

She looked confused. 'But you're Donovan. You're not scared of anything. You managed to tackle a guy with a gun.'

He took a deep breath. He'd never revealed this part of himself to anyone. He hadn't wanted to. He didn't want gossip circulating about him that could affect his position at the DPA. He'd never been prepared to take that risk.

But this was Grace. Someone he felt a connection to. And she'd just put herself on the line for him. He had to be honest with her. He had to let her know that she wasn't alone. He could ask her about the dating stuff later.

'Irrational fears are a funny thing. You're right. Apart from a few jittery nerves, I wasn't that scared of the guy with the gun. I knew if the timing was right, I could overpower him.'

'Then I don't get it. What are you scared of?'

He pointed to the light streaming in from the entry point. Even saying the words made the little hairs stand up on his body. 'I need to know I can get out of places. I had a bad experience as a kid. I was trapped in an elevator for hours. As long as I can see the way out, I'm fine. And in most circumstances I can. Take the exit route out of my line of sight and a whole host of things start churning around in my head.'

She looked horrified. 'That must have been awful. What age were you?'

'Six.'

'And how long were you in the elevator?'

He gave a big sigh. Talking about it brought it all back to him. The feeling of abandonment. The silver walls all around him. Needing to pee so badly it hurt. Crying so hard it made his chest sore. Wondering if he would ever see his mother again.

'Six hours.'

'Six hours? For a six-year-old?' The pitch of her voice rose in obvious shock. This was why he didn't tell people. He didn't want sympathy. He didn't want to relive the horror. He just wanted to put this all in a box and forget about it. Too bad his subconscious wouldn't let him.

'So how do you expect to collect samples at the back of a cave, hundreds of feet away from the exit?' It was the obvious question.

'The same way you expect to collect samples in a cave with no lighting,' he countered.

They looked at each other. For the first time it seemed okay to admit to a fear. They were on an equal footing. One fear overlapped the other.

The temperature in his suit was rising—and it wasn't just down to the suffocating Florida heat. It wasn't quite so stifling in the caves. The air was damper, more humid, but those were probably contributing factors to the spread of the virus.

No. The temperature was rising in his suit purely because of the way Grace was looking at him and the inappropriate thoughts that were clouding his brain. This was what he'd feared. Romantic entanglements with a colleague meant your mind wasn't on the job. And right now his certainly wasn't.

He wanted to run his hands through the tangled waves of her hair. He wanted to feel her skin beneath the palms of his hand. He wanted to feel the warm curves of her body pressed against his.

The hazmat suits made them look like spacemen on an Apollo mission. Nothing sexy. Nothing revealing. And yellow probably wasn't his colour. But Grace? She made anything look good.

She was still staring at him. There were the tiniest beads of sweat along her brow. It just made him want to touch her all the more. Last time she'd had water on her brow had been in the sea, in that orange bikini.

And then she did it. She ran her tongue along her dry lips. It was almost the end of him. He let out a moan that resembled a little growl. Thank goodness there was no one near them. He shook his head inside the hood. 'Grace, don't.'

She lifted her hand, palm open, and held it up facing him. She ran her tongue along her lips again. 'Why, what am I doing?'

She knew. She knew how ridiculous this was. But the buzz of electricity was giving them both the distraction that they needed. Who knew hazmat suits and bat caves could be sexy?

She moved her hand again. 'Okay, Mr Team Leader. We can do this. Together.'

He took a deep breath, willing his body to stop reacting to her every move. For a few seconds at least his childhood fears had been forgotten. He lifted his gloved hand to press against hers. 'Together.' He smiled. 'Wanna hold hands?'

She leaned forward, lowering her voice. 'That's not really what I want to hold. But let's just get this over and done with, okay?'

No. His body was definitely not playing fair. Thank goodness for padded body suits.

He pulled his shoulders back. He had a job to do. Irrational and unreasonable fears be damned.

As for the sexy distracting chat—they could talk about that later. Alone. Naked. Undisturbed. And Grace could hold any part of his body she wanted.

He took long strides towards the back of the cave, turning and following the path far away from the entrance. He didn't think about it. He had a clear way out behind him. He had a torch in his hand to show him the way.

He sensed a little movement at his back. The

light pressure of a hand resting on his suit. Grace was matching him step for step. She was just holding on for the ride.

A flicker in front of him showed him where the ranger had stopped. He pointed his torch in the direction of the bats roosting on the curved roof. The ranger's brow was furrowed. 'What kept you? Did you two get lost?'

Donovan didn't answer. He swung round and held a hand out to Grace. 'I'll collect some samples from the cave floor. You swab the sides of the cave.'

The ranger swung his torch to one corner, lighting up the corpse of a dead bat lying on the cave floor. 'What about that? Do you want to take a specimen?'

Donovan nodded. 'I'll bag it and seal it.' It didn't really matter what had caused the death of the fruit bat. David would still be able to test it and see if it carried the virus. He turned and handed his torch to Grace, waving his arm towards the ranger. 'Can you light up the area for her while she collects samples?'

She shot him a grateful glance. He didn't mind

fumbling around in the dark. It only took a few minutes to collect the samples of bat droppings he required for the lab and to bag and seal the dead bat. Who said this job wasn't glamorous?

'All right, Grace?'

Her hood, lit up by the torch next to it, was casting an impressive range of shadows around the cave. Her outline looked like a monster from a kid's book. The stalagmites and stalactites were all over the deep part of the cave here. In any other circumstances it would be a perfect setting for a horror movie.

She glanced at him. 'What is it?' Her voice wasn't trembling any more. She didn't seem so rattled.

He smiled. He was trying not to think about how he couldn't see the way out from here. It was much easier just to look into Grace's eyes and think about a whole host of other things.

'I was just imagining you in one of those kids' storybooks. You know, the monster in the caves kind of thing?'

'You're just all charm, aren't you?' she shot back. She gave him a little wink. 'I'll make you pay for that later.' His distraction techniques were working.

He stood up and pushed the double-bagged bat into the sample case. 'Are we done?'

She breathed an obvious sigh of relief and nodded. 'Let's get out of here.'

He turned back towards the way they'd entered and gave a little start. Darkness. Nothing in front of him. No obvious way out. Sealed in a million tonnes of rock along with some deadly bats.

He squeezed his eyes shut for a second. He was Donovan Reid. He couldn't do this. In any other lifetime this would be described as a wobble. He couldn't let that happen.

Then he felt Grace lay her hand on his arm. She held out the torch in front of her. He could see she was taking some long, slow breaths. She glanced sideways at him, aware that the ranger was watching them both. 'Let's go.'

She walked first, letting the thin torch beam ahead of her be the beacon lighting the way out. She moved briskly, without talking, until they reached the bend in the cave that revealed the entrance ahead.

He felt all the pent-up air rush out of his lungs. He hadn't even realised he had been holding it. As they neared the entrance his phone beeped loudly. It was inside his suit, it would have to wait.

It took a few minutes to reach the outside of the caves. The decontamination unit was set up outside and they all stripped off their gear and headed for the showers. This time there was no sharing of cubicles. No untoward views of a naked Grace. It was almost disappointing.

He towelled off his hair and picked up the phone. The screen was steamed up and he wiped it clean and stepped outside.

No.

'What is it?' Grace appeared beside him, towel-drying her hair too.

He held up the phone. 'Just what we don't want to hear. Two adult fatalities in the last hour. One at our hospital, another, a late diagnosis, at a hospital in Mexico. He visited the caves last Thursday. John found him during the visitor follow-ups. We need to step up a gear.'

'But what else can we do?'

His eyes skimmed over her body. She was wearing simple clothes. A T-shirt and a pair of fitted trousers. All he could think about was what lay beneath.

It couldn't happen. He couldn't do this.

This was exactly what he'd feared. People depended on him to stop this outbreak. He couldn't do that while his head was full of Grace.

She was watching him with her green eyes. Trusting him because of what they'd just shared.

He kept his tone sharp as he walked away from her. 'Get those samples to David at the labs. I'm going to speak to whoever is in charge of the park. I'm going to get the whole area cordoned off.'

He couldn't turn round. He *wouldn't* turn round.

Because he didn't want to see the expression on her face.

CHAPTER EIGHT

WHAT WAS WRONG with him?

He'd barely spoken to her in the last few days. She was getting more conversation out of Mara from the kitchen than she was from Donovan.

Oh, he mentioned patients and gave instructions. The caves had been confirmed as the site of the virus. The Jamaican fruit bats had been rounded up and taken away while some scientist worked out how the virus had travelled between African and Jamaican bats.

She'd waited the last two nights to see if he would knock on her door. She'd even hesitated outside his door the other night, not even knowing if he had actually been there or not. Then she'd sat in her room, pulled the doors back and stared out at the beach to see if she could spot him running.

It was ridiculous.

Callum Ferguson, in the meantime, was charm himself. He spoke to her for an hour at every handover, praising her work, answering any questions and giving her a few hints about things she was unsure of. She was finally starting to shake off the bad feelings that Frank Parker had initiated. Was finally starting to feel like a valuable member of the team.

But Donovan was doing nothing to help that.

He was sitting at one of the nurses' stations, working on a computer. She wasn't going to avoid him. She hadn't done anything wrong. So she flopped into the seat next to him and picked up the phone.

'Hi, it's Dr Grace Barclay from the DPA team in Florida. I'm just phoning to check on the condition of the kids we sent to you a few days ago.'

She listened carefully, taking a few notes. They had five kids now in other ICUs. Two still very serious and three who seemed to making small improvements.

She replaced the receiver with a sigh. She didn't even care what kind of mood Donovan was in right now. 'Tyler Bates, the five-year-old we resuscitated? He's still not doing great. They've transfused him three times and are giving him extra clotting factors. He's still haemorrhaging.'

Donovan turned his head slightly. 'And the other kids?'

'Obi, Sarah and Mario have made slight improvements. Jenny is still serious.'

He nodded and turned back to his screen.

'Aren't you going to say anything else?' The stats for the Marburg virus were circulating around her head. Anything between a twenty-three and a ninety per cent death rate. They had treated more than thirty kids so far. She couldn't bear the thought of having to deal with a child death. She'd never had to do that before. She was getting angry with Donovan's deafening silence. She stood up, sending the wheeled chair skidding behind her. Her voice rose. 'Do you know that his mom's pregnant? They've forbidden her to enter the isolation room. The risk to the baby is too great. She can't even hold her little boy's hand.'

'Sit down, Grace.' His words were quiet and they just infuriated her all the more.

'No, I won't sit down. I don't want to sit down. I want you to talk to me.'

He raised his eyebrow. 'I am talking to you.'

'No, you're not. Not really.'

One of the nurses hurried past, her eyes flicking from one to the other. She picked up a prescription chart and disappeared into another room.

Donovan took his hands from the keyboard and leaned back in his chair. 'Grace, it's late. We have to hand over to Callum in an hour. I've got another three suspected cases in sites around the world. I'm trying to organise a way to get their samples checked in labs that have no idea what Marburg virus looks like. What do you want me to do? Ignore the work I'm supposed to be doing, to deal with your temper tantrum?'

She stopped dead. 'My what?'

'Your temper tantrum.' He waved his arm at her in exasperation. 'That's clearly what's going on here.'

She was holding back sobs. She walked to the other side of the desk. It was safer. She couldn't punch him from there.

She leaned over towards him, 'What I'm doing, Donovan, is offloading to my team leader. I'm juggling more than twenty paediatric patients right now—an area I don't specialise in. We only have one paediatrician and he's on the other team. I've got another two kids that should ideally be transferred to another ICU, but there are no available beds at Panama Health Care, and if I send them to another facility I'll have to authorise another DPA team to attend.' She drummed her fingers on the desk.

'My brain won't stop reminding me of the death rate for Marburg.' She waved her arm down the corridor. 'We've lost five adult patients now. How long will it be before we lose a child? And will I be left to deal with that too? Because, quite frankly, Donovan, I don't know if I can.' She ground her heels into the floor. 'So, no, Dr Reid, this isn't a temper tantrum. This is a frustrated colleague wondering if she's cut out to be on a fieldwork team. Believe me, if I was having a temper tantrum, you would know it.'

There was a fire in her eyes he'd only glimpsed on occasion before. A fire that made her seem more beautiful than ever. Even after five days here, staying in a backwater motel, her dark hair was glossy and her skin glowing. Grace looked as if she should be on the cover of a magazine.

All of a sudden he couldn't stand it. He couldn't stand it a second longer. His brain seemed to have lost its *don't-say-that* clause. The kind that made you adjust what you really wanted to say to the words that formed on your lips. 'Grace, what's going on here?'

She pulled back. She seemed surprised by his forthright question.

Her brow wrinkled. 'What do you mean?'

He waved his hand. 'This. Us. What is this?' He was confused. It was strange for him, because clarity of thought was one of his great strengths. He just couldn't make sense of this any more.

For a second she said nothing. Her mouth wasn't hanging open, but it was obvious words were stuck in her throat. She sighed and put her head on the desk.

Not the best sign he'd ever seen.

'I've no idea. I can't work it out myself.' Her words were mumbled into the top of the nurses' station and under her waves of shiny hair. She lifted her head, her green eyes fixing on his. For a few seconds he actually felt clear-headed. 'This is you, Donovan. This is your fault. You kissed me. You touched me.'

He half smiled. 'You weren't complaining. In fact, I'm not entirely sure if I did initiate that kiss. It felt pretty mutual.'

'It did. Didn't it?' She thumped her head back down in exasperation then held out her hands. 'Why is this so wrong? Why can't this just be a simple boy-meets-girl?'

'Why do people like Frank Parker exist?' His eyebrows rose automatically. He still felt murky. The lights seemed unnaturally bright. But being around Grace just felt so natural.

She sighed. 'Frank Parker. I hate that. I hate that whether or not I can date someone depends on what some lowlife said on Twitter.'

'Who said anything about dating?'

She looked a little shocked. He hadn't quite meant it to come out like that. It was almost as if someone had taken the safety filters off his brain and mouth. 'Well, no. Of course. I didn't mean that…'

He stood up and put his hand over hers. *Zing.* There it was. Every time they touched. For a second he felt a little light-headed. Had he swayed? Just as well there was a barrier between them, because right now he just wanted to take delectable Grace in his arms and pull her close to him. It was like this whenever they were around each other. As if some invisible force just pulled them together.

'I don't just want to date, Grace.'

There. He'd said it out loud. It went against every one of his principles. It went against every instinct to protect her from gossip. It went against his deep-rooted fear about not being on the ball at work because he was too busy thinking about a colleague. But he just couldn't help it. He had to say it out loud.

His sensibilities didn't seem to be in place today. He was thinking with his heart and not his head.

His heart. His brain was definitely stuffed

with cotton wool today because he never thought things like that.

But how else could he describe it? Grace had lighted up his world these last few days. Every smile, every flick of her hair, every sway of her hips. All he could think was that he didn't want this to stop.

He didn't want to go home to an empty apartment every night and a dog who looked at him as if he'd been abandoned. Because that was just it, it didn't really feel like a home. Even Casey wasn't filling the gap that was there.

Was this what love felt like? Donovan wasn't sure that he knew. Attraction to the opposite sex had never been a problem. Raging hormones had never been a problem. But this was a whole lot more than that.

He didn't just want to have sex with Grace. He wanted to have a relationship with her. He wanted to make her smile. He wanted to make her happy.

He'd never even tried anything like this before. Maybe that's why part of his brain kept screaming no. He didn't want to do anything to hurt

Grace. He didn't want to do anything to make her vulnerable. If anything, he wanted to protect her.

He could feel heat rising in his skin. It felt stranger than before. Different from the usual effect of being around Grace.

There was a flicker of something in her eyes. He squeezed his shut for a second. The lights in here seemed even brighter than before. It was relief. Relief that he'd acknowledged the obvious attraction.

Kissing seemed like the obvious way to acknowledge it, but saying it out loud made it real.

'I don't know what it is about you, Donovan Reid,' she said softly, looking at his warm hand over hers. She shook her head slightly. 'I just know that in the last few days I can sense whenever you're around, whenever you're near me.' The edges of her lips turned up by the tiniest margins. 'This has to be real. Donovan. I don't do this. I don't feel like this around men. Not in a long time.'

Something clicked inside his brain. 'Since the attack?' His hand subconsciously squeezed hers.

'Especially since the attack. I haven't really felt safe around any man since then.'

'And around me?'

'It's different. You're different. We're different.' It was almost as if she couldn't meet his gaze again. They were in the middle of a ward. Other staff were wandering around. 'What happened in the caves…' Her voice tailed off.

'You've never told anyone that before?'

She shook her head. 'No.'

'Neither have I. A team leader who doesn't like not having a clear exit route? It isn't exactly ideal. Who knows where we could end up? It makes me feel like a liability rather than a valuable member of staff.'

Words. Words he'd never thought he'd say out loud. What was wrong with him?

She nodded in acknowledgement. 'We make an unlikely pair.' She drew in a deep, haltering breath. This time she did meet his gaze. Voices were starting to echo round about him. Noises increasing in volume then fading just as quickly. 'I know you have reservations, Donovan. But you've just admitted you feel exactly the way that

I do. We're not Sawyer and his first wife. What happened to her was terrible, but that doesn't mean it's ever going to happen again. The DPA has made provisions for that. We could give this a chance if we wanted to.'

He could almost hear her holding her breath—waiting for his response.

But he couldn't think clearly. It was easy to focus on Grace and the overwhelming feelings he had towards her. But he was losing perspective all around him. This couldn't work. It just couldn't. She was still waiting for his answer. The expression on her face was pained. He blinked. It was almost as if she was surrounded by fog.

Things were starting to feel unreal. Like some weird dream. He had to try and take some sense of control again. His vision was blurring. Was this what not eating did to you? Made you feel so muggy and unfocused?

He tried to straighten his thoughts. He wanted to tell Grace how he really felt about her. He wanted to tell her how much he hadn't wanted to leave her room the other night, how all he'd really wanted to do had been to push her back onto the bed and feel the softness of her skin on the palms of his hands.

But the words just couldn't form on his lips. Grace was a wonderful doctor. The last thing she needed on her first fieldwork trip was distractions. She needed a chance to make her mark on the team in her own right. Not with whispers and rumours surrounding her. He had to step back. He had to step away from her. He had to protect her.

'No, we can't. We can't give this a chance, Grace. It has to stop here. It has to stop now. From this moment on it has to be a strictly professional relationship. Nothing else.' She was shifting in his gaze, coming into focus then blurring. He had to be clear as he possibly could. 'I don't want anything else.'

Her face crumpled and she spun on her heel and strode down the corridor as fast as her legs would carry her. If she stayed a second longer she couldn't be held responsible for her actions.

It was the way he'd just looked at her. As if nothing had ever happened between them. As if he'd never run his fingers over her skin, never felt his lips on hers.

He'd looked at her as if she were just a regular team worker he'd had no connection with at all.

And it cut her to the bone.

She'd been the one to walk away. She'd said at the beach that it had been a mistake. But he'd been the one to come to her motel room. He'd been the one that had kissed her as if he never wanted to leave.

Then, after what had happened at the caves…

She knew now. She knew him. And there wasn't another person on the team who knew what she did about Donovan. Likewise, he was the only person to know about her inbuilt fear, the one she was trying so hard to get past.

Whether he liked it or not, they were connected. And she felt it. Every single time she was around him. No matter how much he ignored her.

How could he not be feeling it too? Because this didn't feel like a passing fling. This didn't feel like some silly one-night kiss. This went deeper than she'd ever experienced before, running through her veins, tugging completely at her heartstrings. Every time she saw him her heart gave a little leap, her skin went on fire and her senses on red alert.

It was like a constant adrenaline surge. She couldn't eat. She couldn't sleep. She just thanked God she was still doing a good job. Because right now it was the only thing that was working in her favour.

Donovan felt like crap. His head ached, his muscles were sore and he felt as sick as a dog. He glanced at his watch again. Callum was due in a few minutes. Thank goodness. Right now every minute felt like an hour.

Grace was mad at him. And to be honest, he probably deserved it. When she'd snapped at him he just hadn't had the patience. But she was right. About everything.

He should have been supporting her more. He knew this was her first fieldwork assignment and she'd more than proved her capabilities already. Dealing with sick children was always more difficult for any team member. Dealing with kids who had a virus with a potentially high death rate was another thing entirely.

He should have taken the time to have a private discussion with her about what had happened between them. He could have done this so much better.

He should go after her. But then he might say something inappropriate like he loved her. He couldn't do that. He couldn't risk her position on the team. And right now he just didn't think he could get his body to move. His legs felt like lead and he rubbed his eyes as the words on the computer screen seemed to dance around him.

'Donovan? Donovan?' The voice grew sharper.

He felt fuzzy. He definitely needed to sleep. Or maybe he needed to eat? When was the last time he'd eaten? But his stomach was churning. He couldn't face the thought of food right now.

'Donovan.'

The voice was right in front of him. David thumped into the chair next to him and shook him by the shoulders. 'What's wrong with you?'

David leaned forward, then immediately pulled back again. 'Are you sick?'

'Just tired. I need to sleep.'

'No. It's more than that. What are your symptoms?' The voice was direct and intense. David might work in the lab but he was a fieldwork member could fill any role on the team. He wouldn't hesitate to take any actions he needed to.

Donovan stretched out his back, trying to loosen his sore muscles, and went for his natural automatic response. 'I don't have symptoms. I'm fine.'

Or maybe he did? His brain started to straighten out. What were his symptoms?

It was as if a thousand little caterpillars started marching over his skin with ice-cold feet.

He couldn't have contracted the virus—could he?

No. He'd been wearing protective gear since he'd got here. Any patient contact he'd had he'd been fully covered. As for the caves, he'd worn the full hazmat suit. Nothing got through that.

The chills continued. The resus case. He hadn't been wearing full protective clothing for that. He'd pulled on a pair of gloves but that had been it. A child hadn't been breathing, and he'd prioritised.

He'd had to maintain Tyler's airway and the little boy had already been haemorrhaging. Truth was he'd probably been exposed to all kind of body fluids.

'I want to draw your blood.' David's voice had never sounded so firm.

Grace. He needed to talk to Grace. He needed to apologise and give her more support. He didn't have time for this.

David was walking around now, in and out of treatment rooms, collecting supplies. Before Donovan could argue, a tourniquet had been tightened around his upper arm and David was tapping the skin in his inner elbow.

'Stop it. What you are doing?'

David ignored him. 'Do you feel sick, nauseous? Have you had any diarrhoea? Sore head, scratchy throat? Any chills or a rash?'

He slid the needle under Donovan's skin with the ease of long experience then started slotting on the collection bottles for the various samples of blood.

Donovan didn't know whether to be mad or grateful. And that told him everything he needed to know.

'When do you think you could have been exposed? We've been here just over five days. You must have been exposed at the beginning.'

His head was pounding. He had to stop thinking like a doctor. For once in his life he had to play the part of a patient. 'No sickness, no diarrhoea. Yes, I have a headache, a sore throat and some chills. But that could be a hundred other things.'

He opened his eyes to face David's grey ones and the mask covering his face. It gave him a jolt. His colleague was taking no chances.

'The resus,' he finally said. 'I could have been exposed at the kid's resus. It was five days ago. Maybe a little bit more.'

David finished collecting the samples and pressed a cotton-wool ball into the crook of Donovan's elbow. 'Hold this.' He glanced up and down the corridor. There were approaching footsteps.

'Callum, I've just taken a sample from Donovan. He's having some symptoms. Can you arrange for him to be put in an isolation room until I get some results?'

The air turned blue with Callum's Scottish expletives. He didn't hesitate and moved straight over to Donovan. David thrust a gown and gloves towards him and was met with another outburst of words.

Donovan was fine. He was absolutely fine. But any second now he was going to be sick all over his shoes. And this fuzzy headache made him feel as if he was surrounded by a huge cloud of cotton wool. Words and pictures were disorientating him. Like any person, he'd had sickness bugs before in the past, but this didn't feel like a normal bug.

Callum's loud voice carried up the corridor as he sorted out a bed. Among all the voices and confusion there was only one clear thought in Donovan's head. Only one thing he could focus on. Grace.

He wanted to talk to her. He wanted to touch her skin and run his fingers through her hair. He wanted to sit down face to face with her. He wanted to tell her that everything about her confused him. He'd never been so distracted by a woman in his life.

He'd never had that gut-clenching feeling about a woman before. She could make him smile just by walking into the room. She played in his thoughts every day and every night. And no matter how much his gut told him that dating someone in the team was a bad idea, every other part of his body disagreed.

He squeezed his eyes shut and he could see her walking out of the sea in her orange bikini with the water streaming from her body; he could see her striding across the concourse at the airport with her wraparound dress and newly found confidence.

He could see the hurt and fire flash in her eyes when she'd been mad at him earlier. Why hadn't he spoken to her? Why hadn't he gone after her?

'This way, Dr Reid. We have a room ready for you.' One of the nurses was at his elbow. Totally gowned, gloved and masked. Infection-control procedures were in place.

Oh, no.

He'd kissed Grace. He'd definitely swapped

body fluids with her while he'd been incubating the disease. He'd put Grace at risk. He felt a sharp pain in his chest as if someone had just grabbed hold of his heart and squeezed tightly.

No. Not Grace. Anyone but Grace.

'Callum!' He had no idea where Callum was but he had to tell him. The nurse at his elbow jumped as she tried to lead him down the corridor. Panic seized him. This was what he'd dreaded. This was what he'd always feared. And he'd been right.

He was finding it difficult to focus, difficult to concentrate. Grace was the one solid picture in his mind. His head was thumping, it felt as though the pulsing blood supply was echoing around his brain. This wasn't normal. It wasn't right.

Thumping footsteps and a heavy hand on his arm. 'Donovan, what is it?'

'I kissed Grace. I kissed her.' He couldn't hide the desperate tone in his voice. Neither could he make out Callum's reply. The world around him was swimming, hazy lights merging and blackening, the strangest feeling flooding through his body as all energy seemed to leave him, turning his legs to jelly.

Then everything went dark.

She was eating the greasiest, unhealthiest pizza in the world. She'd been so mad she'd left the hospital without eating and had found out to her peril that Saucer Boys Pizzas was the only option near the motel. The bad punctuation should have told her everything she needed to know.

The grease wasn't helping the horrible feeling in the pit of her stomach.

The horrible feeling that she'd made a terrible mistake.

She pulled open the doors to the beach, drinking in the ocean view and releasing some of the odour of toxic pizza.

The plastic white chair on the tiny balcony was designed to be uncomfortable. What she'd really like to be doing right now was sitting with a glass of wine in hand, watching the sunset on the horizon. But she wasn't in that Zen-like kind of place.

She was too worried about the kids. She was too worried about doing her absolute best on her twelve-hour shift tomorrow. She was too worried she might miss something important.

She was too worried about Donovan and her actions around him.

There. She'd let that thought into her crowded brain. It almost felt like some of the other thoughts were there deliberately, trying to push him into the background and pretend he wasn't important, when the truth was he was centre stage in her brain all the time.

Donovan didn't want to be involved with someone at work. End. Of.

It didn't matter that he'd told her he was attracted to her. It didn't matter the way his body reacted when they kissed. It didn't matter that the man could glance at her from the other side of the room and set her skin on fire.

This wasn't going to happen.

The long and short of it? Donovan was right.

She was too busy thinking about him to focus on her job. Her cheeks flushed with embarrassment and her eyes felt wet instantly.

She had a horrible sinking realisation. She was

in that first flush of love. The kind that made you dizzy and lose focus.

Shouldn't love make you shout from the rooftops and sing to the world? Wasn't love supposed to make you happy and view the world through rose-tinted glasses?

Not when the person who held your heart in their hands had just told you there was no chance for you.

She buried her face in the pillow on the bed. It didn't offer any comfort as it was hard and impossibly lumpy. She had a horrible feeling of dread. As if there was something else—something more—and she just didn't know what.

The sooner she got out of there the better.

The door knock sounded sharply. She jumped and glanced at her watch. Then her heart started to flutter. Donovan. It had to be Donovan.

She stood and crossed the room quicker than she'd thought possible. Her hand hesitated at the doorhandle. This was it. This was where she had to admit to exactly how she felt about him. This was where she had to put her hand on her heart and tell him that he was right.

Dating the boss was never going to work. She was beyond distracted. She wanted to love everything about this fieldwork post, but all she could think about was Donovan.

Until she'd been in this position she could never have imagined how it felt.

Maybe there would be a chance to join another team. Maybe if she could wait it out a little longer, she would have opportunity to decide where she wanted to specialise and move to another department.

That could work. It would be time limited. They could have a no-touch policy for a few weeks—or, at worst, a few months. Surely they could last that out?

Her heart gave a little surge. It wasn't hopeless. It wasn't. This could work.

She pulled open the door. 'Donovan, I was just thinking that—'

Except it wasn't Donovan. It was Callum Ferguson. His large frame filled the doorway. Thank goodness she was appropriately dressed.

He leaned against the doorjamb, folded his arms and gave her a crooked, knowing smile. 'So, Dr Barclay. You kissed Donovan Reid.'

'What…? Who told you that?' She wasn't quite sure how to respond. Her first reaction was to deny it. But Callum was already looking at her as if he could read her mind.

She couldn't quite get over the fact that Callum was standing on her doorstep. He was the last person she'd expected to see.

But there was something else. The usual twinkle in his eyes wasn't there. Was he mad? She felt a little shiver go down her spine. Callum didn't look mad. This was something else entirely.

'What is it?'

He sighed and ran his fingers through his grey hair. *What wasn't he telling her?* 'Donovan had to tell me he kissed you, Grace.'

'Donovan told you? But why?' Her mouth started working before her brain. Why on earth would he try and get them both into trouble? That made no sense. No sense at all. Unless…

'Oh, no.' Her hand flew up to her mouth. Unless Callum needed to contact trace. Her public-health head could put the pieces together a whole lot quicker than her Donovan-filled brain.

'What's wrong? What's wrong with Donovan?'

Callum's firm hand rested on her upper arm. 'Grace, calm down. I know you only finished work a few hours ago but I think it would be best if you come back to the hospital.'

There was serious edge to his voice and she was ominously aware that he hadn't yet told her what was wrong with Donovan.

'Of course.' She crossed the room quickly, slipping her feet into her shoes and picking up her jacket and bag. 'Let's go.'

It was only a five-minute drive back to the hospital. Her brain was in overload. She was trying not to acknowledge the fact that Callum had obviously left the hospital to come and get her. They'd been getting one of the hospital maintenance staff to pick them up and drop them off before this.

She was trying too hard to keep control. The fact that Callum knew she'd been kissing Donovan seemed irrelevant. The initial embarrassment had only taken a few seconds to disintegrate into the wind with the thought that something was really wrong.

She'd been feeling a little melancholy before. Realising the strength of her feelings for Donovan, and his attitude, which had seemed unreasonable before, was probably for the best.

The car pulled up next to the ambulance bay of the hospital, a little cloud of dust rising around them as it screeched to a halt.

She jumped out and waited at the door for Callum. He didn't waste any time, striding down the corridor and heading towards the lab. 'Come with me,' he called over his shoulder.

She bit her lip. 'Where's Donovan?' But he didn't reply and she sucked in a breath so quickly it hurt.

She hurried after his disappearing frame. For a big man, Callum could move quickly. He lifted the phone outside the laboratory entrance and buzzed the staff inside, putting them on speakerphone. Everyone was wearing a hazmat suit, and there were three staff. Was Donovan in there?

All three heads turned. David, John and Lucas from the other team. No Donovan. She winced.

'Is anyone going to tell me what's going on?' She was starting to feel desperate. As if there was some unspoken rule that no one could tell her what was wrong. There was still the horrible feeling in the pit of her stomach. The reason that Donovan would have to reveal personal information to Callum, to allow the public-health duty of contact tracing to take place. But why wouldn't someone just put her out of her misery and tell her?

David looked up from his microscope, his eyes darting past her and fixing quickly on Callum. The man she'd shared a few jokes with earlier now couldn't look her in the eye. 'I can't find any evidence of Marburg virus in his sample. No shepherd's crook. Even if it was in the early stages there would still be some evidence in the sample.'

Callum nodded. 'Best guess?'

John walked over to the glass panel. 'While you've been gone I've been up and taken a lumbar puncture. I think we've got a meningitis case. Give me an hour.'

Callum nodded. 'I'll start him on some IV antibiotics in the meantime. I'm not going to wait on the results.'

He touched her elbow. She felt numb. Numb with shock. She'd thought Donovan had been off with her earlier. She'd had no idea he was ill. What kind of a doctor was she if she couldn't pick up symptoms in a colleague?

'Grace? Do you want to come back upstairs with me?'

She nodded and followed him to the stairwell. Donovan must be seriously unwell if they'd first suspected Marburg virus. Meningitis was every bit as serious and some of the symptoms were similar to Marburg. The headache, sore neck and throat, temperature and nausea.

Her legs were moving quicker and quicker. She couldn't help it. More than anything in the world she wanted to see Donovan. She wanted to know that he'd be all right.

As soon as they exited the stairwell she could see a flurry of activity at one of the rooms at the end of the corridor. She couldn't stop herself and started to run.

Callum matched her step for step. 'What is it?' he asked the nurse inside the room.

Her face was pale. 'A rash. It's started to appear across his abdomen.'

Her eyes met Callum's. They didn't need to say a word. Both of them knew that in some cases of meningitis, by the time the rash appeared it was too late for the patient.

Donovan was lying on the bed, his face coated in a sheen of sweat, his eyes closed. His chest was bare, the definition of his toned arms clear. She walked over to the side of the bed and touched his damp hair. His skin was burning. 'Donovan? It's Grace. Why didn't you tell me you were feeling unwell?'

He didn't move. He didn't respond. Not even a flicker of acknowledgment. She turned to the nurse. 'How are his observations?'

The nurse frowned. 'His level of consciousness has deteriorated quite quickly. I've put him on neuro obs. His blood pressure is dropping and he's pyrexial.'

Callum walked over to the nearby trolley. The nurse had already just brought out some antibiotic supplies. He pulled up a bolus of cephalosporin into a syringe, looked at the clock on the nearby wall and started administering it directly into the venflon on Donovan's hand.

Grace couldn't help herself. She pulled the thin sheet back from Donovan's chest. The tiny red and purple-hued petechial spots seemed to be materialising before her eyes. She knew exactly how serious this was. She grabbed his hand. It was colder than the rest of his body. He didn't even flinch when she squeezed his hand. Her eyes went to the clock as she watched Callum slowly push the first dose of antibiotics into Donovan's vein. She was trying to do some calculations in her head. This seemed to be a very rapid onset. Was it some kind of bacterial meningitis? She could only pray that he didn't become septicaemic, with all the complications that could ensue.

She looked around her and pulled up a chair. She didn't care what else was going on. She was going to stay here by Donovan's side.

She met Callum's gaze and stared hard. She

would say the words out loud if she had to. She didn't care who heard.

He finished administering the antibiotic and reached across the bed, putting a hand on her shoulder. His Scottish accent was heavy, the way it always became when he got emotional. 'I've contacted the DPA. A replacement team is on their way.' He looked down at his colleague. 'He needs a CT scan. There isn't one available here. He's also going to need ITU facilities.'

She nodded as a single tear snaked its way down her cheek. She couldn't bear the way his hand didn't feel the way it had the last time it had touched her body. It was clammy, cold. It didn't feel like Donovan's hand. Not the warm hand that had stroked her skin. The lack of response from him was more than disturbing.

She picked up his chart. 'Can we give him some steroids before we arrange the transfer?'

Callum nodded as he picked up another glass vial and started pulling the liquid into a syringe. 'On it.' He hesitated. 'Grace, do you want to go on the transfer?'

'Yes.' She didn't falter for a second.

She didn't care what anyone thought. Although it helped matters greatly that none of the team had commented at all. In fact, most of them seemed quietly supportive. She didn't doubt that Callum had shared the information about them kissing. He'd had to. If they'd first suspected Marburg virus, they had to know Donovan's every contact.

Would there be repercussions now their kiss was out in the open? They were two consenting adults, it was hardly criminal behaviour. But she already knew relationships between team members weren't really approved of. If she was going to be allowed to remain in fieldwork she would be transferred to another team. That had become the norm after Sawyer had lost his wife.

Callum injected the steroid slowly. It would be hours before they had an official diagnosis. But in suspected cases it was always the case of treat first, ask questions later. Cases of meningitis had been known to kill in twelve hours.

It didn't matter that it would probably be a helicopter transfer and she'd never been on one before. She didn't care that even the sound of helicopter rotors made her nervous beyond belief.

All she could focus on was the man lying on the bed next to her and the fact the last words she'd said to him had been in anger.

The phone rang shrilly outside. One of the nurses darted out to answer it. The other came and fastened the blood-pressure cuff around Donovan's arm.

Grace gave her a smile. 'Don't worry. I'll do his observations. I'm going to be here anyway.'

'Dr Ferguson, that's Panama Health Care about the transfer to ICU.'

He paused in the door way and gave her a resigned sort of smile. 'Don't worry, Grace. Donovan will be fine.'

She could only pray he was right.

CHAPTER NINE

ONE FRANTIC HELICOPTER transfer later Grace was beginning to lose hope.

Donovan's blood results had gotten steadily worse, edging closer and closer towards septicaemia. His blood pressure had bottomed out, his temperature had shot sky high and he'd needed assistance with his breathing. His body was in shutdown and she didn't need anyone to tell her that.

Not the nurses that hovered around his bed, not the machines that alarmed at all times of the day and night, not even the admin assistant who'd told her where she could find some clean scrubs and a shower.

She didn't want to leave his side. She *couldn't* leave his side.

Callum was always phoning the ICU. Another team had arrived to assist in Florida and things were under control at the hospital. She was glad. Because right now she couldn't focus on anything but Donovan.

Was there really a huge difference between Callum Ferguson, the Granddad of Disease, not being able to focus on his job and her? He might not be sitting by her side, but he seemed to know every one of the staff members on the unit on a first-name basis.

She shifted in her seat again. The worst part of all of this was that sinking feeling in the pit of her stomach that Donovan had been right all along.

When the worst had happened, she'd fallen to pieces. She hadn't been able to function. She'd been unable to focus. There was no way they could work on the same team in the future. No matter what happened between them. She couldn't go through this again.

His hand twitched and she was on her feet immediately. He'd had a few involuntary muscle spasms in his legs but nothing like this.

The accessory muscles around his chest started to move and his eyes flickered open. Panic. He was sensing the ventilator and starting to panic.

'Nurse!' she shouted. 'He's waking up.'

The nurse was at her side in an instant, obviously used to dealing with the clinical situation. She adjusted some dials on the machine and leaned over Donovan, speaking softly.

'Hey, Dr Reid. I'm Marcie, one of the nurses here. You have a little tube down your throat to help you breathe and some medicines to try and assist you. How would you feel about getting that tube out? Can you blink for me or give my hand a squeeze?'

Donovan blinked as if his life depended on it and the nurse called over a colleague. They sounded his chest, whilst Grace waited impatiently at the side. His sedation, which was already minimal, was stopped, the ventilator disconnected. And after a few painful coughs from Donovan the tube was removed.

Grace shifted nervously as the nurse blocked her view. She was still talking quietly to Donovan as she adjusted his position on the bed and gave him a few tiny sips of water to help his throat.

After the longest five minutes of her life she finally moved and gave Grace a smile. 'We'll be doing fifteen-minute obs and one of our medics will come and check Dr Reid over. Would you like me to give Dr Ferguson a call?'

Callum. Of course. The old devil had charmed all the nurses in here with his thick Scottish accent. 'That would be great, thanks.'

She pulled her chair closer to the bed and sat down next to Donovan, waiting for the nurse to be out of earshot before she spoke.

Feelings of pure relief were washing through her. He was awake. He was conscious. His temperature was coming down and he'd been extubated. A few hours ago she'd feared the worst.

She took a deep breath and tried to appear casual. 'Well, you certainly know how to cause a commotion.'

He leaned forward and lifted his arm, taking a sip of water through the straw on the table placed in front of him. His voice was dry and throaty. 'It's a special skill.'

He sagged back against his pillows. Just taking that drink had looked like a gargantuan effort.

She smiled. It was definitely Donovan. He was back. There was a slight tremor in his hands and he was definitely pale and thinner, but she'd never seen someone look so good.

'Are you going to tell me what happened?' His voice was strained.

She waved her arm out, 'Welcome to Panama Healthcare ICU, Donovan. It seems that taking over the kids ICU wasn't enough for us.'

Deep furrows lined his brow. 'I had Marburg?'

She wondered how much he would remember. Meningitis could have lasting effects—sometimes even brain damage. But Donovan appeared to have all his faculties and was just trying to orientate himself.

She shook her head. 'No. You didn't have Marburg—though they did suspect it at first. You had meningococcal meningitis.'

'Me?' He looked incredulous. That was a danger of working in a fieldwork team. After a while the team members—no matter how good their training—started to think they were impervious to certain diseases.

'You.'

'What type?'

There were lots of different strains of meningitis. 'W135.'

'But I've been vaccinated against that.' He rubbed his hands over his face as if trying to make sense of all the facts. The staff at the DPA were vaccinated against everything they could be.

'And that's probably why you're still here. You and I know that vaccination isn't infallible. If you hadn't been vaccinated things could be a whole lot different.' She couldn't hide the shiver down her spine. She was trying to talk like a fellow professional, giving him the information he needed to fill in the gaps in his head, but her body was reacting in a much more personal way.

'But where on earth could I have caught that?'

He was thinking out loud. She could tell straight away. He really didn't need a response. 'Do you want me to write you a list, Dr Reid?'

His eyes met hers. There was still an element of confusion in them. His muscles would ache from lying in that bed and his throat would be sore for days. She felt his eyes drift up and down the length of her body.

Her hands went to her hair self-consciously. She hadn't washed it in three days. She'd barely washed her face. Any trace of make-up was absolutely gone. She'd had to steal some deodorant from one of the nurses on duty and this was her third set of scrubs. Navy blue was certainly not her colour.

'Grace, how long have you been here?' He looked around him. 'How long have I been in here?'

Wow. She must look bad.

She took a deep breath and plastered a smile on her face. 'Three days.'

'Three days?' His voice echoed around the unit and every head turned in the direction of his exclamation.

She put her finger to her lips. 'Shh. Yes, three days.'

'But what about the Marburg? What about the patients? Who is looking after them? Are there enough staff? Why aren't you there?' The words came tumbling out of his mouth with no pause to take a breath.

There was a tiny sinking feeling of dread in

her stomach. His questions were entirely natural. He wanted to make sure everyone was okay. But the last one was hurtful. The last one made her think that he saw her as nothing more than a colleague.

Maybe he hadn't remembered what had happened between them. Maybe she'd imagined that first twinkle in his eye when he'd woken up.

She bit her lip and tried to answer as methodically as possible. 'They flew in another team. David and John are still working with Callum. There's been another adult fatality but no child fatalities from the Marburg virus in the last few days. Two new cases have been identified elsewhere.' Her voice faltered a little and she wondered if he noticed. She was trying to take into account the fact he'd just woken up after being really ill. She was trying to remember that his body would be exhausted, having fought off meningitis for three days. She really should leave him alone to rest and sleep.

But she couldn't. She hadn't had anything to think about these last three days but him. No matter how she examined her feelings about him, or her reactions to him, it all came down the same thing. Donovan had been right. This couldn't work.

She met his gaze. He still looked pretty dazed. 'Why do think I'm here, Donovan?'

She left the question hanging in the air between him. It took a few seconds for him to react. Almost as if the little jigsaw pieces were fitting into place in his brain.

His eyes widened. 'I told Callum. I told him about us.'

'You did.'

His head started shaking. 'I had to. I had no idea what was wrong. I just couldn't think straight. I could have hurt you. I could have infected you with something.'

She gave the slightest shake of her head and pointed to a plastic container of meds on his bedside locker. 'I've been given antibiotic cover.' It was normal for close contacts of patients with meningitis.

She licked her lips. She'd already made her decision. She knew what she had to do. All she had to do was press Send on the email.

She couldn't keep working with Donovan. If anything like this happened again, she'd never be able to concentrate on the job they were there to do. It wasn't fair to the patients and it wasn't fair to the other staff members. Watching his chest rise and fall for the last three days had brought that home to her.

Being attracted to someone was one thing. Acting on it another. Feeling as if your life would end if theirs did was something else entirely.

She'd cried every time his blood pressure had dropped or temperature rose. Not doctor-like responses, not professional responses, but from-the-heart responses.

He closed his eyes for a second and rested back against his pillows. It was obvious his body was exhausted. It would be another few days until he would be well enough to be discharged. 'I'm sorry, Grace. I never meant for this to happen. I never meant to put you in harm's way.'

'You didn't. I'm a big girl. I did that myself.'

He opened his eyes. 'What do you mean?'

'I kissed you right back.'

She saw the flicker behind his eyes. But it didn't seem like emotion, it looked like regret.

'You were right, Donovan. You said people who work together shouldn't be emotionally involved. And I didn't get it. I didn't get it until Callum turned up at my door and told me you'd collapsed and were unconscious.' Now she'd started she couldn't stop. 'I felt as if someone had reached into my chest and squeezed my heart with both hands. I've spent the last three days and nights worrying myself sick over you. I've even fielded calls from your dogsitter.' She shook her head.

'But you were right. I can't work like this.' She waved her hand towards him. 'We can't work together. It's no good. I need the chance to see what a fieldwork team is like without complications like this.'

Was she connecting with him? She just couldn't tell. And the wave of hurt washing over her was getting stronger by the second. She had to get out of there.

He was safe. She knew he was safe. It was time to walk away before she embarrassed herself.

She stood up and reached out and touched his

hand. It was a mistake, and she knew that instantly. The zing shot up her arm and she pulled it back to her chest.

'I've requested a transfer to another team. I think, under the circumstances, the director will approve it. I hope you feel better soon.' Tears were pooling in her eyes, the heat in the room clawing at her chest. She needed to get out of there.

He moved, his hand reaching towards her. Every part of him looked exhausted. The best thing she could do right now was let him rest. He started to speak, 'Grace, I…'

But she wasn't listening. She needed to get away. She didn't want platitudes, she didn't want to add excuses to the mix. She would chalk this up to experience.

She picked up the bag at her feet and headed to the door. The wash of cool air was an instant relief. The doors in the distance took her to the outside and her feet powered down the corridor.

Out of the hospital. Away from the claustrophobia of the unit. Away from the pain in her heart.

* * *

Donovan's befuddled brain definitely wasn't working. He threw back the thin sheet on the bed and tried to move his legs. It was like having the body of an eighty-year-old. They edged towards the side of the bed in slow motion. One of the nurses appeared at his side. 'What do you think you're doing?'

He pointed in the direction of the door. 'Going after her.'

The nurse looked at the swinging door and sighed. 'What did you say to upset her? She's sat here for the last three days and nights, breaking her heart. If that's not a sign of a woman in love, I don't know what is.'

His heated skin felt chilled. Everything about this was going so wrong. When his eyes had flickered open and Grace had been sitting at his side, everything had felt right in the world. Even in the midst of his confusion, as he'd tried to make sense of things around him, knowing Grace was right next to him had grounded him.

She was his anchor. His place in this world. She was the last thing he'd thought about when he'd been ill, and the first person he'd seen when he'd woken up.

But he'd hurt her. Without even trying to. His brain and mouth didn't seem to want to engage together.

But all of a sudden it was as if a symphony of light appeared around him. 'It's what I didn't say.'

The nurse raised her eyebrows. 'Say what?' He tried to stand and she pushed him back firmly. 'No way. Tell me what you need to say to her. I'll catch her in the corridor.'

He shook his head and gave her a rueful smile. 'I need to tell her that I love her.'

The nurse blinked then waved her finger. 'Oh, no. That you have to do yourself. Give me a sec.' She disappeared behind the nurses' station and came back with a phone in her hand. 'What's her number?'

He must have looked blank. 'Her number. I know she has a mobile phone because she charged it at the station.

'Oh, right.' He racked his brain before hesitantly reciting out the digits of what he hoped was Grace's number. The nurse pressed them in and held the phone to her ear for a second. She held it out towards him. 'It's ringing. Go on, then, Dr Reid. Just call me Cupid.'

The sun was blisteringly hot. Her three-day-old clothes were scrunched up in a plastic bag at her feet and long beyond redemption. She hadn't given much thought to walking about outside the hospital in scrubs. It was hardly ideal.

The bag on her shoulder gave a little buzz. It took her a second to realise it was her phone. She'd turned the ringer off while she was inside the ICU.

She fumbled around and pulled it out. Unrecognised number. She pressed the button and held it her ear. 'Dr Grace Barclay.'

'You didn't let me finish.'

A deep throaty voice. Donovan. Where on earth had he gotten a phone? 'There isn't anything else to say.' Her breath was caught in her throat and her heart fluttering in her chest. How could he have this effect on her?

'Yes, there is. I love you, Grace. I don't want you to walk away like this. I want to talk.'

She felt herself sag against the wall. 'But…'

'But nothing.' His voice was raspy. It must be paining him with every word.

'I love you, Grace Barclay. I get what you say about the work thing. My first thought when I realised something was wrong was that I might have infected you too. I couldn't live like that, Grace. And I might be right, but I'm wrong too. I can't just walk away. I can't pretend that I don't think about you every minute of the day. You're what I want, Grace. You.

'I don't care about gossip. I don't care about talk. I want to protect you. I want you to love working at the DPA. I want you to grow and flourish and for everyone else to see what Callum and I already have—that you're a great doctor. I don't want to get in the way of that We can find a way to make this work. There's always a way to make things work.'

Her brain was whirring, trying to absorb his words. The three little words she'd wanted to hear. The three little words she'd admitted to herself but not said out loud.

'Grace? Say something. Please. Anything?'

Her heart was fluttering in her chest, the corners of her mouth creeping upwards. He'd said it. He felt it too.

The barriers were down. All bets were off. This was about him and her.

'I love you too, Donovan.'

There was a cheer in the background from the phone. 'Who was that?'

'The nurses. Now, can you come back so I can kiss you?'

'I think I can manage that.'

EPILOGUE

One year later

THE DREAM HAD turned a little strange. The waves lapping up on the beach weren't clear blue water any more but something kind of rough and soggy.

'Casey!' She sat up in bed and pulled her hand back from where Casey had been licking it.

She turned but the bed was empty, a hollow in the mattress showing Donovan had only just got up.

Things had worked out perfectly. Grace was now a member of Callum's team. No drama, no gossip. With the director's blessing she'd simply done a swap with another member of staff.

Casey jumped up onto the bed, trying to burrow in beside her. It was his new favourite trick. 'Get off.' She laughed as she pushed him away, noticing his collar had been replaced by a big red bow.

'What on earth...?'

She pulled Casey onto her lap. He tilted his head to the side, staring at her with his big brown eyes. After a few months of tiptoeing around her, with some disdainful doggy stares and some huffs, he'd finally accepted Grace into the family.

'Well, who looks very pretty?' She looked around either side of Casey's head, her fingers catching on something attached to the ribbon. There was a tag.

She snapped it off and read the card.

Will you be my new mommy?

Her breath caught in her throat as her fingers felt something else attached to the ribbon. Something with a bit of sparkle.

'Donovan?'

He appeared around the door with a tray in his hands.

'Casey! You were supposed to wait for me.'

He laid the tray at the end of the bed. 'I think I'm supposed to be in this position when I ask this.' He moved down onto one knee next to her side of the bed, his grin stretching from ear to ear as one hand moved over and rubbed Casey's ear.

He unfastened the red ribbon and laid the ring in the palm of his hand. 'Grace Barclay, I love you with my whole heart. You're the woman who can always show me an exit route, and you definitely hold the key to my heart. Will you marry us?'

She leaned forward and wrapped her arms around his neck, 'Will you say that in our wedding vows?'

'That you always show me the exit route?'

She nodded and placed her hand on his chest. 'And you always light up the dark for me.'

'I like the sound of those vows. Is that a yes?'

'That's definitely a yes.' And Casey gave a yelp as the two of them rolled over on the bed and landed on top of him.

* * * * *

MILLS & BOON®
Large Print Medical

March

A SECRET SHARED...	Marion Lennox
FLIRTING WITH THE DOC OF HER DREAMS	Janice Lynn
THE DOCTOR WHO MADE HER LOVE AGAIN	Susan Carlisle
THE MAVERICK WHO RULED HER HEART	Susan Carlisle
AFTER ONE FORBIDDEN NIGHT...	Amber McKenzie
DR PERFECT ON HER DOORSTEP	Lucy Clark

April

IT STARTED WITH NO STRINGS...	Kate Hardy
ONE MORE NIGHT WITH HER DESERT PRINCE...	Jennifer Taylor
FLIRTING WITH DR OFF-LIMITS	Robin Gianna
FROM FLING TO FOREVER	Avril Tremayne
DARE SHE DATE AGAIN?	Amy Ruttan
THE SURGEON'S CHRISTMAS WISH	Annie O'Neil

May

PLAYING THE PLAYBOY'S SWEETHEART	Carol Marinelli
UNWRAPPING HER ITALIAN DOC	Carol Marinelli
A DOCTOR BY DAY...	Emily Forbes
TAMED BY THE RENEGADE	Emily Forbes
A LITTLE CHRISTMAS MAGIC	Alison Roberts
CHRISTMAS WITH THE MAVERICK MILLIONAIRE	Scarlet Wilson

0215 LP 2P P1 Medical